D0428875

ADVANCE PRAISE FOR

RED MENACE

"*Red Menace* is a compelling and engaging story of a tumultuous and painful time in our history. Through a young boy's eyes, we are drawn into the experience of a particular family, in that time and place. Marty Rafner is a character with great heart and depth. Lois Ruby accomplishes that rare feat of sparking an interest and enticing the reader on to ask questions, dig deeper, and learn more."

—Clare Vanderpool, author of *Navigating Early*
and Newbery winner *Moon over Manifest*

"Lois Ruby brings the divisiveness of the Cold War era to life through the experiences of a thirteen-year-old Kansas boy. Like many boys, Marty Rafner cares only about baseball and its heroes, but he's forced to contend with the realities of McCarthyism and its effects on the nation and his own small town. We watch Marty discover new heroes and perhaps become one himself. This is a powerful work that will touch the hearts of young people and alert them to a troubling time in our nation's history."

—Rabbi Michael Davis, whose grandfather, Rabbi Abraham Cronbach,
delivered the eulogy at the funeral of Julius and Ethel Rosenberg

RED
MENACE

Lois Ruby

CAROLRHODA BOOKS
MINNEAPOLIS

Carolrhoda Books®
An imprint of Lerner Publishing Group, Inc.
241 First Avenue North
Minneapolis, MN 55401 USA

For reading levels and more information, look up this title at www.lernerbooks.com.

Jacket illustration by Alexandra Bye.
Paper background: Stephen Rees/Shutterstock.com.

Main body text set in Bembo Std.
Typeface provided by Monotype Typography.

Library of Congress Cataloging-in-Publication Data

Names: Ruby, Lois, author.
Title: The Red Menace / Lois Ruby.
Description: Minneapolis : Carolrhoda Books, Lerner Publishing Group, [2020] | Summary: "During the summer of 1953, thirteen-year-old Marty's parents are suspected of communist sympathies, upending his life and causing him to question what it really means to be a patriotic American" —Provided by publisher. Includes historical notes.
Identifiers: LCCN 2019000738 | ISBN 9781541557499 (lb : alk. paper)
Subjects: | CYAC: Communism—Fiction. | Cold War—Fiction. | Surveillance—Fiction. | United States. Federal Bureau of Investigation—Fiction. | Jews—United States—Fiction. | F   20th century—Fiction.
Classification: LCC P.

LC record available at

Manufactured in the U
1-46157-45954-9/11/2019

70832878

FOR MY TWO 2020 BAR MITZVAH BOYS,
JACOB AND MAX

"I think about baseball when I wake up in the morning. I think about it all day and dream about it at night. The only time I don't think about it is when I'm playing it."

—RED SOX CENTERFIELDER CARL YASTREZEMSKI

"The Rosenbergs were familiar. To a child the connection was unavoidable: if they could be executed, what was to prevent the execution of one's own parents, particularly one's own mother? . . . [I] can still summon the terror— and the fury at my mother for risking her life, the utter despair . . . She must have sensed then that what she and my father were committed to—that progressive political dream they'd lived together—had become a nightmare."

—AUTHOR CARL BERNSTEIN

CHAPTER 1
THURSDAY, APRIL 16, 1953

L ast week the FBI pulled up across the street and aimed binoculars at my house. At Amy Lynn's next door, too. They're staking us out round the clock, like we're Mafia bootleggers.

Hey, G-men, I've got news for you. Al Capone doesn't live in the neighborhood. This is Palmetto, Kansas, not Chicago, Illinois. No dead stiffs lying around on Oxbow Road.

They won't notice anything suspicious about me, Marty Rafner, the world's most loyal Yankees fan. Right now I'm innocently shooting hoops with my best friend Connor Dugan, who lives down the block, though the FBI's not checking out his family.

Connor has his big butt in the air as he dives into the sage hedge to get the ball. Jabs his finger on one of those thorny things, so he pops the finger into his mouth, sucking blood.

"Shoot!" I holler. Connor flubs a one-hander wide of the basket. "Jeez, you never even came near the pole."

"Basketball's not my game. I'm a baseball man."

"Yeah? Well, don't forget, Mickey Mantle played football and basketball in high school, not just baseball."

Connor puffs up. "But I pour all my talent into one game. First string, shortstop. Let's see, where are you? Oh, yeah, way out in center field. You need a telescope to spot the ball." He shoots.

"Whoa. That one hit the rim. You're missing closer."

"Hey, Marty, how bad you think it hurts when they shoot that electricity through you?"

The Rosenbergs. They're always lurking in the back of our minds. Even if my parents *didn't* know them personally and *didn't* make them the hot topic at our dinner table, the daily radio bulletins would keep reminding us about their upcoming execution.

I don't respond, but Connor just won't ice it. "Think it feels like your insides are fried? Two eggs, sunny side up?"

It's like a jolt of current is racing through my own gut. I shoot and miss. "Nah, I think it's more like you're zapped with a stun gun." Dribble, dribble, lay-up, my signature shot, like I practiced a million times. A million times, and I still overshoot the rim.

"You kidding? They'll be flopping around for about six minutes."

My shot bounces off the board and streaks past us into the street. Under the G-men's car. "Go for it, Con."

"I'm not messing with the FBI!"

Am I gonna sacrifice a decent basketball, or wait a month or a year until they give up and go home?

They make it easy for me by starting up their Studebaker and crawling a few feet up the block, freeing the ball so I don't have to belly my way under their car. But as soon as I've got my prize, the car backs up into its same old rut.

I swear, Connor's got a one-track mind. "Wonder if they'll sit next to each other, like a two-seater electric chair. Picture it, sparks flying back and forth, *zowie*."

My stomach roller-coasts.

"Bet you two bits Julius and Ethel will holler like banshees when that shock whizzes through them. Pshoooo." Revved up by this picture, Connor sinks one and sends the rim vibrating.

I snag the ball smack out of the net and glance across the street at the Everlys', where Luke's not. Luke used to dribble about fifty times before shooting. Where's he now? On a transport, heading home from Korea with a Purple Heart. Might not be able to stand up, let alone shoot baskets.

Man, don't I know anybody whose life is toodling along happily? Amy Lynn's family is getting the same attention from the G-men that mine is. That's about everybody on our block—the Sonfelters, the Dugans, the Everlys, and us, the Rafners. Oh, and a few other neighbors I only see when I take the trash cans out to the street. Mom calls them the Garbage People.

I pull the ball to my achy chest, hugging it like the earless stuffed chimp I used to stash under my pillow. "Those two boys, both their parents will be dead on the same day. Think about it, Con. How would you feel?"

"Parents like that? They sold us out to the Ruskies. We're talking A-bomb secrets."

"Aw, come off it. They never gave the Russians any secrets, on account of they didn't have any to give." My parents and all their Hawthorne professor buddies swear that the Rosenbergs are not spying traitors. A lot of people think they are, though. Doesn't matter one way or the other anymore, does it? Appeals denied, date set, boom. Zap.

The U.S. Supreme Court's refused to hear the Rosenberg case twice already, and the execution date is circled on Mom's kitchen calendar. Doomsday, June 18. Only two months away.

Connor lives for that day. "My father says their kind, Julius and Ethel and Amy Lynn's father, they'll turn us all into a whole country of pinkos."

My lip curls up to the left, like Mom's when she hears things that tick her off, and a lot of things do. Around our house, *pinko* is a lip-curling cuss word. So my lip's practically wagging like a tail, and I can barely get the words out. "The Rosenbergs were framed, Con, and you know it. The trial was a circus, the judge was crooked, the star witness—Mrs. Rosenberg's own brother—man, he lied on the stand to get his wife out of hot water."

"Well, my father says if they're commies, that's good enough for him. The only good red's a dead red." Like his father's such an expert. Mr. Dugan's the head of buildings and grounds at the College, but he's got louder opinions than half the faculty.

Connor shoots again. The rim rattles and the ball bounces off.

I snag it. "You're all heart, Con. Get this: the Rosenbergs are not guilty!" I pound my gavel-fist full force on the basketball. Needs air. So do I, trying not to picture Michael and Robby shooting baskets in some other driveway, knowing their parents will both be dead before their next birthdays.

Connor snorts. "Not guilty, huh? That's what they all say on Death Row." He does a staggering number, gasping with his last breath, "I'd rather . . . be dead . . . than red. Aaarggghh." Keels over in the grass, belly up. Great for bouncing the basketball off his flabby gut.

I don't want to talk about the Rosenbergs anymore. It'll be a relief when June 18 finally rolls around and the whole thing's over, and the Yankees are hotter than lava, and the Mick is batting .330, and life is ordinary, white-bread, Kansas normal again.

"Shoot!" I yell again, knocking the wind out of Connor with a basketball bomb to the solar plexus.

"Hey, you trying to kill me?"

"It's tempting."

Connor laughs, but I'm semi-not kidding. I guess my anger inspires him, because he jumps up and sinks two in a row.

CHAPTER 2
FRIDAY, APRIL 17

It used to be so easy with Connor and me. We didn't even have to talk; just knew what was up. But everything's different now, since the FBI poked their noses into our lives. Who's left I can count on? Old faithful, Mickey Mantle. No doubt about it, the Mick's still my man. I don't write him memos anymore, though. Not since a couple years ago, when I decided it was dumb for a guy hitting fifth grade to scratch notes to some other guy who wouldn't read them anyway, even if I'd had the guts to drop them in the mail. Which I didn't.

But here I am dragging the shoebox full of memos from the top shelf of my closet. Why now? What's the FBI got to do with the Mick? Nothing, although I'm starting to think nobody's safe from their clutches, and man, the feds sure went after Jackie Robinson a few years back.

The house is quiet this afternoon. It used to be swarming with students from everywhere from Athabasca to Zurich—which, if you asked me to find them on the map, forget it. Some nights I'd wake up to their shouting. I'd trundle out to the hall. Cigarette smoke would be coiling up the stairs, and I'd hear them rant about some guy named McCarthy. Not Charlie McCarthy, the ventriloquist, and not Joe McCarthy, the manager who'd taken the Yankees to four consecutive World Series in the '30s. *That* would be worth getting fired up about. No, they were ranting about Joe McCarthy, the Wisconsin senator, the one known around our house as the Lie-Mongering, Red-Baiting Carnivore, since he eats up peoples' lives. Turn over every rock, the Carnivore says, and you'll uncover a cowering communist red menace.

It's tough being the son of two college profs, especially the doctors Rosalie and Irwin Rafner. Other families sit around the dinner table talking about I Love Lucy, or about whether you squeeze the toothpaste tube from the top or the bottom, or whether there was an air raid drill at school. Not my mom and dad, the superbrains who turn a warm meal into a hot debate.

Everyone in my family has strong opinions, except me—unless it's about baseball.

Far as I can see, the only great part about being a professor is these neat memo pads with my dad's name printed in green ink. Just the size I needed to keep the Mick up to date on my baseball team, right? Har-de-har, like he was dying to know.

The memo pad didn't take much doctoring to make it mine, like this first one:

DATE: August 29, 1951

TO: Mickey Mantle

Man, what a rookie season you're having, a bat outta
H-E-Double Toothpicks. So just when everybody
(mostly me) was figuring you for Rookie of the Year,
you go and hit a slump and get yourself booted
down to the Triple A farm club. Hey, I know about
slumps. Look the word up in Webster's, and it's got
a snapshot of me: Martin Weitz Rafner, known on
the field as Marty el Magnifico. You haven't heard
of me? Gimme time, and you will, because by seventh
grade I'll be the lead-off batter for the Palmetto
Pirates JV's. Won't take long until the scouts
discover me, like they did you down in Oklahoma.
And if you believe that, you'd believe chickens had
eyelashes. Hey, wait, this just came over the radio.
They're bumping you back up to New York, and you'll
be wearing Number 7. Great news for all the sevens
in the world.

Your friend,
MARTY

See what I mean? What a birdbrain. So, I'm thinking of making confetti out of the whole shoebox full of
memos. Then I'll soak the pieces in Clorox and toss the
pulpy mess at the Palmetto dump before the G-men grab
all my family's personal stuff, like they did to Amy Lynn's
family. It's happened to other people we know, too. Some
of them are locked up. Look at Mr. and Mrs. Rosenberg,
cooling their heels in Sing Sing. On Death Row.

A couple of months before they went to jail, their
family came to our house for dinner when they were
in town for some sort of meeting over in Wichita. It
was before my tenth birthday. Michael and Robby were
younger than me. If I'd known they were about to be
accused of espionage, I might've expected people like
movie stars, all fancy-dressed and snooty and full of
snappy stories.

Later, I racked my brain trying to remember how
they'd acted at the dinner table—if they'd said or done
something courageous or at least interesting, but they
were just a regular Jewish family like us.

I remember Mr. Rosenberg gazing out of those little
round glasses that made his eyes look as big as ping-pong
balls. "Splendid pot roast, Rosalie," which it wasn't,
because my mother is a poet, not a cook. She could win
the Nobel Prize for Shoe Leather.

Michael, the bigger kid, was chawing on a slab of
pot roast speared on his fork when Mrs. Rosenberg hollered, "Put that meat down, Michael!" Next thing, his

little brother Robby, who was so small that he had to sit on two phone books, accidentally knocked a glass of apple juice across the table, which sent us all laughing like hyenas, and that was my first clue that everybody was super nervous, and that this *wasn't* normal company in our home.

I never saw them again, but they sure get a lot of air time at our house.

Yeah, so what *about* Michael and Robby, who'll be losing both their parents when the guy with the black hood throws the switch? One switch for two?

Man, it's just not *healthy* for a guy my age to personally know people who are gonna fry in the electric chair on June 18. That's—wait, let me count—sixty-two days from today. Yikes.

CHAPTER 3
FRIDAY, APRIL 17

I'm sitting with Amy Lynn on my front steps after school, shifting around for a shady spot. I don't have much experience talking to girls, my mom being the only other one I know pretty well, and Amy Lynn Sonfelter's not at all like Mom. Mom's all sharp cheddar, but Amy Lynn's as smooth as Velveeta. See where this is going? Nowheresville, because she's already fourteen, and my thirteenth isn't for a few days. She's always saying, "Marty, you're the little brother I never had." Man, I should have been born two years old.

Like Luke Everly used to say before Korea, back when he was teaching Connor and me how to do layups, "Love is cruel, but it beats hate by a long shot, kiddos."

In a minute Amy Lynn's gonna have to cross the street to babysit Carrie when Luke's wife, Wendy, goes to work at the college library. To get up the courage to pass the FBI car, Amy Lynn focuses a pair of binoculars at the G-men. It's Spy vs Spy, right out of *Mad Magazine*. "I'm watching them watch us, and they don't even know it. The short one with the dimpled chin is snoozing. Look at his blubbery lips. See?"

She swings the binocs over. I catch a whiff of her shampoo, which smells like strawberries. Do girls wash their hair in Tutti Frutti gum?

Must stink in that Studebaker across the street, though, both of them sweating all day and takeout left-overs rotting on the floor. About every three hours they drive over to the Shell station, so at least there aren't buckets of pee fermenting in the back seat.

Amy Lynn says, "At breakfast this morning, my father slapped the picture of Senator McCarthy in the *Sentinel* and hollered, 'This is the scoundrel responsible for framing the Rosenbergs and for all our woes, he and his wretched posse of hate committees.'"

"Hear that a lot at my house, too, only we don't mention his name. We just call him the Lie-Mongering, Red-Baiting Carnivore."

Amy Lynn's voice drops to a whisper. "My pop's in big, big trouble, Marty. The College suspended him, without pay, for not signing the loyalty oath. Don't they realize that he was Teacher of the Year in 1951 and 1952? What's worse, they've given his classes to Dr. Muldaur, who was never once nominated. But Muldaur will sign anything. He'd probably confess to murder if they asked him to."

"What happens now?"

Amy Lynn sighs deeply. "No one knows. They've been poring through Pop's personal papers for a week now. They won't find anything besides a lot of math formulas, unless they plant something incriminating."

"I wouldn't put it past them."

"Maybe Pop could get a job teaching at the high school, but he's ridiculously over-qualified. It would be laughable if it weren't so horrible. Or I suppose we could just starve. Go on welfare and end up buried in paupers' graves."

"One of my parents' friends got fired from KU 'cause he wouldn't sign a loyalty oath," I offer. "He moved his family to Mississippi to teach at a Negro college, and he's not even a Negro. He's Japanese."

"No! I'd just die if Pop did that. I'd be so lonesome for everything here."

For me?

"Oh, Marty, can't you just imagine how Julius and Ethel Rosenberg must be lonesome for each other, locked up in opposite ends of Sing Sing?"

I was thinking more about how scared they must be. The Chair, the electric chair waiting for them.

But Amy Lynn's the romantic one. "I saw a picture of them in *Look Magazine*. They're on their way from court back to prison. Ethel's hooded eyes are gazing into Julius's with such longing that you could cry. You can see how she adores him and yearns for him, even though there's chicken wire separating them in the patrol wagon. It's utterly heartbreaking."

She sharpens the focus in the binocs. "What's that

drooping out the window? Oh, it's Dimple Chin's tie. He's going to wake up with a stiff neck. Serves him right!"

"Maybe his head'll snap right off and roll under the car like my basketball."

Amy Lynn's giggle is like ripply water. She sighs and cranks back into gear. "I've heard that Julius and Ethel pass their time in their cells writing passionate letters. They've convinced guards to carry the letters back and forth."

"Bribed?"

"*Bribed!* Where is your romantic spirit, Marty? They do it out of sympathy for those poor lovers. I've read a few of the letters leaked to the papers. Steamy prose! If I were Ethel I'd be so embarrassed." She lets the binocs hang from the leather strap around her neck.

"Don'tcha think Ethel has bigger stuff to worry about, like staying alive?"

"Yes, but love conquers all," Amy Lynn says, in this faraway dreamy voice. "So, I wonder, just how deep does love go? Deep enough for them to hold hands walking down the corridor to the electric chair? How do they decide who goes first?"

I jump up and take a sweeping bow. "'Ladies first,' Mr. Rosenberg will say, and Missus will say, 'No-no-no, after you. Age before beauty.'"

"She's older."

So much for my attempt at humor.

"I've heard that all Ethel has to do to save herself is admit that Julius is guilty. But she won't. They'd rather die together than live without one another. That's my dream."

"To get electrocuted?" What's she *talking* about?

"No, to love somebody that much, some day, and be loved back. They're like Romeo and Juliet, like Abelard and Heloise."

"I get the Romeo thing, but who are those other guys?"

Amy Lynn slaps her hand to her heart, making the binoculars bounce like a ping pong ball. "You never heard of Abelard and Heloise? Where have you been, Martin Rafner? They're just the most classic lovers in the whole history of the world, or at least in the drafty stone castles of the twelfth century."

"Even more famous than Joe DiMaggio and Marilyn Monroe?"

She gives me this disgusted look. How come Amy Lynn's always lecturing me on the stuff I don't know? How come I don't know so much stuff?

She tilts her head northward, toward the campus. "Of course, Romeo and Juliet both turned up dead, and I won't even tell you the horrible fate of Abelard and Heloise. Love is so, so tragic, Marty."

"Kinda like losing the World Series," I say.

Told you I don't know how to talk to girls.

CHAPTER 4
SATURDAY, APRIL 18

Even before the FBI guys showed up, our family wasn't like other people's families. My professor parents are called *doctor*, but they couldn't set a busted leg or gouge out your appendix.

I always knew my dad was different from other fathers. For one thing, he doesn't go nutso over sports like Connor's dad.

It's not that Dad has no sports sense. He's an anthropologist, so he knows more than anybody on this planet about sports in a dozen countries you never heard of. Amazing what you can do with coconut shells and wooly mammoth spine bones.

Also, my mom's not like other mothers. "Housewife?" She always huffs, "I am not married to a house. I'm married to a profound man, and I'm a superb English professor and poet in my own right. Housewife, indeed!"

Explains why you'd think our house has been ransacked by thieves.

Connor's always here at lunch time, and he's always

hungry. Maybe he has a tapeworm swimming around in his gut, like some of the people in countries Dad studies. He drops into his usual seat at the kitchen table.

"Don't get your hopes up," I warn him. I've got my fingers crossed for Campbell's Tomato Soup, but no such luck. Mom's clunking a pan of something. Truth is, Mom dishes up her best stuff in moronic pentameter. I think that's what her students call it when they come to our house for poetry readings and leave their teeth marks in half-eaten crackers with cream cheese and chopped olive smeared on them—stuff you'd use to grout bathroom tile.

She splats barefoot across the floor to the window sill, where her avocado pit is sitting in a mayo jar with its round bottom submerged in water. "I *dare* you to grow roots, you imbecile pit." After she's turned it to face the sun, she ladles thick white sauce with mysterious beige flecks onto soggy toast.

"This chipped beef?" Connor asks, his hungry eyes gleaming.

"Tuna. Chipped beef in cream sauce isn't kosher," Mom says. Not that we keep all those dietary laws, or that we're super-religious, but Mom was brought up not mixing meat and dairy, and whatever meat we have comes from the kosher butcher in Kansas City so when Bubbie Sylvia comes to visit, she's okay eating our stuff. Creamed tuna is second on my Hit Parade of worst meals. Pickled tongue tops the charts. The sight of a package of oatmeal-raisin cookies on the counter cheers me a little, even though I don't like raisins or oatmeal.

Connor goes to work on the creamed tuna like a stevedore who's been hauling at the docks all morning. Me, I stab at the wreck on my plate. "Don't they put food in your cage?"

"I'm a growing boy."

"Shows."

Mom's more distracted than usual. Probably composing some epic poem in her head with lots of words nobody gets. "Your father had a meeting at the College."

I dig out a green foreign substance, while Connor flicks his tongue across his lips like a gecko. "One of Dad's committees?" They meet at weird hours, like no one at the College gets hungry at normal times.

Mom shakes her head, and that simple tilt of her brownish-gray braid makes me feel itchy. Something's up.

She scritches the bottom of the pan, emptying the gluey blob onto Connor's plate. "Listen, when your father comes home, don't ask him too many questions."

"How many's too many?"

Eyes closed, Mom sucks white sauce off the ladle. "Wash up the dishes when you're done, will you, Marty? And Connor, you'd better be gone before Dr. Irwin comes home."

Connor freezes with his fork half way to his mouth. A wedge of toast and white sauce defies gravity. "This about the Rosenbergs?"

"Indirectly." Mom tosses the white-coated ladle into the sink.

I haven't said a word to her about Connor's hard line on the Rosenbergs, so it must be something else, something big and hairy, if it's got my mother flinging spoons.

Connor spins his plate on the counter and sends the screen door banging behind him, just as Amy Lynn comes in, glaring at his back. She and Connor are sworn enemies.

Mom's at the fridge with her back to us. Her thick braid ends in a little paint brush at her waist. "How's your father doing, Amy Lynn?"

"Oh, he's just peachy-keen," she says dryly. "And my mother's even worse."

Water splashes in the gluey pot. "What's going on?" Mom asks.

"Things are a little tense at my house." Amy Lynn's voice is wobbly. "My mother drifts around the house in an old herringbone sweater she found in the back of the closet, even though our house is steamy and dark as a cave, with every window shut and the blinds down so those men in the car across the street can't see in."

Mom sighs. "Privacy is dead in America."

"I know!"

So do I. Last night I woke up and saw one of the night guys with binoculars hanging around his neck, trying to climb a tree outside my window. Not that Mom and Amy Lynn bother to include me in this conversation; I'm The Invisible Man.

"Would you believe it, Dr. Rosalie? Those FBI agents rummage through our *trash*. And they leap out of the car when poor Mr. Oberon arrives. They make him show every piece of mail before he can slide it through our slot."

I clunk the giraffe salt and pepper shakers together to get their attention. "Dumb question. All this is happening because your father refuses to sign a loyalty oath at the College?"

"Outrageous, isn't it?" Amy Lynn answers.

"He's got to resist." Mom pounds the table so hard that the salt shaker giraffe jumps and snorts salt out his nostrils.

"Oh, my father's like a boulder. He can't be moved an inch. He won't sign, and he won't tell why he won't sign, except he says it's a matter of conscience."

"Absolutely!" Mom affirms. "It's the only thing left after they strip all our rights away."

"Except it's making Mother furious. She yells, 'Conscience! You're a math teacher, not political science or philosophy. Sign the ridiculous oath and stop this right now!'" Amy Lynn turns to me, with her eyes blazing. "Just wait, Marty. It'll happen at your house, too."

No chance. We've got enough going on with the Rosenbergs. My parents know better than to go looking for even more trouble. Don't they?

CHAPTER 5
SATURDAY, APRIL 18

Amy Lynn is washing, I'm drying. She flicks soapy water at my face, so I have to snap the soggy dish towel at her or look like a dwonk. Outside, gravel's crunching in our driveway. My dad. Uh-oh.

He opens the door just enough to poke his head in. "Anybody here?"

"Marty and me, Dr. Irwin. The Human Trash Can's gone home."

"So sorry to miss Connor." Sweat tracks down Dad's cheeks, gray as oatmeal, and dribbles through his reddish-black beard until it pools at his neck. He's tugging at the tie and starchy collar, his stuffy College uniform. His pinkie sports a Harvard class ring, his only jewelry, not even a wedding ring matching Mom's thin gold band from their poor days.

So, these are the rich days? You couldn't tell by looking at our peeling wall paper and the nicks in the countertops.

The kitchen's half-doors swing open, like in a

western saloon, and Mom comes barreling in. No six-shooter; she's got a finger tucked in the middle of a book and a pen woven into her hair.

"Irwin? Tell me."

Amy Lynn and I go into slow motion with the dishes so we can spy on their conversation. She lazily scrapes a pink Brillo pad over the scummy sauce pan, and I wipe each dish until it's dry enough to spontaneously combust.

Mom stares at my father, who shakes his head, and Mom slams the book down on the table. "They fired him? Unbelievable. Theo's given his life for the College."

Amy Lynn pivots, flinging pink soap. "My father's fired, not just suspended? Mother's going to have a complete cow."

All I can think is, they'll be out of here by fall, off to Mississippi or Timbuktu. There goes my future. See, if by some ugly twist of fate I don't make the Majors, I'm planning to live here in Palmetto, coach baseball at the College, and raise a whole dugout full of little Rafner basemen and basewomen. I kinda thought it would be with Amy Lynn Sonfelter, who wrote in my middle school yearbook, *Yours till the ocean wears rubber pants to keep its bottom dry.* If that's not a promise, I don't know what is.

"They had no choice," Dad says. "Theo's being called up before the HUAC."

Amy Lynn sinks into a chair, dripping soapy water on the speckled linoleum. "What exactly is that, Dr. Irwin?"

Dad lets out a sigh. "It's the Congressional House Un-American Activities Committee—the twentieth-century Inquisition."

Mom adds bitterly, "Railroaded by the Lie-Mongering, Red-Baiting Carnivore and his fascist buddy. They've twisted innocent lives into the so-called red menace by labeling people as communists. Deplorable, unconstitutional, and just plain revolting."

"But my father's not a communist!" Amy Lynn hesitates. "Is he?"

Dad's response is icy and tight: "Not everyone called up to testify is a communist."

I jump in. "Okay, some are, but not Amy Lynn's dad." But all of a sudden it dawns on me. "Wait, even if they just say he's a communist, it's bad for the College, right?"

Hawthorne College is the sun in our universe. Without it, we'd freeze up and turn into a whole neighborhood of flavorless Popsicles. So it's a jolt to hear my father say, "The point isn't what's good for the College—or even whether Theo Sonfelter is a communist or a Soviet stoolie or whatever McCarthy calls Americans with a conscience. The point is a man's political associations are his own business. The First Amendment guarantees it."

"First Amendment, hah!" Mom mutters, taking a swig of milk right out of the Borden's bottle. I'd be grounded if I did that. "And what's next, Irwin? Are we all going to have to sign loyalty oaths? That's blatantly un-American!"

Dad says, "We live in dangerous times. Look at how many of our compatriots are in prison."

"That is not going to happen to my father." Amy Lynn slumps in the chair. Her toes reach my leg, and she doesn't even pull them back.

Mom pats Amy Lynn's arm. "Certainly not."

Dad's not so optimistic. "Extremely dangerous times. Think of the Rosenbergs. Who would ever have thought it would go so far?"

"Yes, and look at the protest marches all over the country," Mom reminds us. "All over the world. Einstein—the president of France—the pope, for God's sake. They're all protesting. And so will we. It's Jewish to protest. We've got to fight this loyalty oath thing, Irwin."

My stomach lurches, like when a line drive comes slamming right to me and I'm scared I'll miss it. Last summer we drove out to New Jersey to visit Bubbie. My parents went to a "Clemency for the Rosenbergs" protest in Newark.

Bubbie Sylvia had a conniption fit. "Listen, sweetheart, your mother and father are very smart people, college professors, no less. But they're crazy-*mishooga* to get involved in such a thing. Believe me, they could wind up in jail. Alcatraz, yet, like that Morton Sobell friend of the Rosenbergs. I should visit my daughter in Alcatraz? I'd drop dead on the ferry across."

She usually cracks me up, but this was no laughing matter. That night I stared up at the ceiling wondering how you could crash-land in jail for trying to get two people out of jail who didn't belong there in the first place. I was still awake at three-thirty in the morning when Mom and Dad finally came home. Phew, no handcuffs.

Now, in our kitchen in Palmetto, Dad nods. "It's a witch hunt, that's what it is. Amy Lynn, I don't know how much this has been discussed in your house."

"Nothing's discussed. They just yell at each other."

So Dad and Mom explain it all to her, which goes something like this: The Lie-Mongering, Red-Baiting Carnivore is the Wisconsin senator, Joe McCarthy, and his fascist buddy is J. Edgar Hoover, the director of the FBI. What a winning team. They're convinced that we're all victims of a red menace, except for the human reptiles like Amy Lynn's father, who ARE the red menace in person. Those traitors are under direct orders from Moscow, the capital of the Soviet Union, to take over the U.S. and turn us all into godless robots who can't keep a dollar we earn because all the money has to be shared with the rest of the godless robots.

Man, that's a pretty grim picture. How do the

26

Carnivore and the Fascist ever get to sleep worrying about stuff like this?

I go back to drying dishes. It's safer—until a plate slips out of my hands and breaks into three even pie slices. No one even looks up while I crawl around on the floor dabbing at crumbs of glass with a wet napkin.

CHAPTER 6
SATURDAY, APRIL 18

Dad asks, "Do you children understand what democracy is?"

Amy Lynn pretends to be totally excited by the topic. Maybe she really is; it's her family's doom.

I need baseball stats to get me through Dad's lecture. Let's see, '52 Series, Yankees and the bums from Brooklyn meeting for the eighteenth time . . . "Yeah, Dad, yeah. Democracy means people vote, and the majority rules." Straight out of my social studies book. I must have been awake for a few minutes in Mr. Mundy's class.

"Majority rules and protects the minority," Mom reminds us.

"We're Jewish, we're a minority, but nobody's protecting my father," says Amy Lynn.

"Precisely," Dad agrees. "And how would you define capitalism?" Pop quiz time, which Dad's famous for.

Slumped down in my chair, with my chin nearly clipping the table, I answer in a monotone, "Everybody's out to make a buck." Yankees sure lucked out getting Mantle. He hit .345 in the '52 Series, nipping at the heels of Gene Woodling with his .348 . . .

"I guess you've stripped both ideologies down to the bone, Martin."

Is that a smile flickering across Dad's face? But in an instant he turns professor again. "Under capitalism, there are the haves and the have-nots."

"Which are we?" I eyeball our kitchen, with the gas stove older than Mom. Two burners haven't worked in years. To turn the oven on, you have to stick your head in with a lit match. On television, stoves light up with the turn of a switch. Like the electric chair at Sing Sing. I squirm in my chair, and a cottony clump of stuffing puffs out of a ripped seam. Amy Lynn follows my eyes around our kitchen to the cooking grease that darkens our ceiling. Her kitchen's so spic-and-span you could do surgery on her table.

I want to be in my room with the radio blasting the game, Yankees vs. Senators. It's the Mick's second anniversary with the team, and I've got an itchy palm, which means he's going to do something colossal. I could have already missed it while I sit here plastered to a hot, sticky chair. Could be the Mick's not playing tonight, since his son was born a couple days ago. It's a sure bet he's never going to be lecturing Mickey Mantle, Junior about commies. Those two, they'll talk baseball ten hours a day and play hit-and-catch the rest.

Gotta get this lecture over with. "Okay, Dad, tie the whole thing to Joe McCarthy."

Dad summarizes: "In a nutshell, McCarthy's ruining lives, children. A lot of lives."

"My parents' and mine, that's three right there," says Amy Lynn. "Especially if we have to wear disguises every time we go to the five-and-ten."

So, the '52 Series victory made Casey Stengel only the second manager with four back-to-back championships. The first was, yep, the other Joe McCarthy . . .

I miss Mom's next few words and tune in when she says, "The HUAC bullies will ask your father to testify about whether he's ever belonged to a communist organization. Doesn't matter what he says. Everybody thinks *guilty* if you're called up to testify, and guilty by association if you're friends with one of these defendants."

That jolts me. "You mean, people will think we're communists because Dr. Sonfelter teaches with you guys and lives next door?"

Amy Lynn scowls at me. "Well, thanks a lot, Marty!"

"Enough for tonight," Dad promises. "We'll just watch how all this plays out."

Mom hugs Amy Lynn. "We're all overwrought. And you, Marty, do you have homework this weekend?"

"Did it all." Except for math and earth science. Oh, and a sonnet thing for English. And some stuff for my bar mitzvah.

"Then do whatever's on your agenda. A baseball game, I suppose," Dad says wearily.

Amy Lynn goes home, and I leave my parents with their elbows on the kitchen table and hang-dog looks on their faces.

Sprawled out on my bed, I can't concentrate on the game. My mind keeps floating toward Amy Lynn's sad, scared face. If that's what communism will do for me, no wonder the Carnivore is against it.

The lights of passing cars stream across my walls, and my hand makes up its own mind and turns the volume knob on my radio, which is always tuned to the station to pick up Mel Allen, Voice of the Yankees, whenever my New York guys are playing. How much have I missed? The radio's all static, and the tuning knob doesn't clear it. Wait, it's not static. It's the sound of 62,000 people holding their breath, and then I hear Mel Allen telling the big story.

Mantle's coming up to the plate . . . switch-hitter's batting right this time. Yogi Berra's on first, Billy Martin's on third . . . Lefty Chuck Stobbs is on the mound for the Senators. Here comes the pitch . . . fastball right to Mantle's sweet spot . . . he swings . . . it's a tremendous drive deep into left field! Going, going, it's over the bleachers and into a yard across the street . . . gotta be one of the longest home runs ever hit! "How about that!" Mel shouts.

I crank up the radio full blast, and I'm dancing around the room like I'm on red-hot coals.

Mantle runs the bases head down, faking it's nothing special. Nobody knows where the ball stopped. Wait, the Yanks' PR guy, Patterson, he's pacing it off. He races out of the park with a tape measure. The crowd's on their feet . . . going wild when Mantle crosses the plate.

My radio's gonna explode with all this excitement. Connor, are you listening to this game at your house? We've gotta play this moment over a million times. Here comes Patterson with the news: Man, that ball rocketed 565 feet!

Mom pounds on my door. "Turn it down. We can't hear our own argument."

I lower the volume and listen to Mel Allen tell about the lucky ten year old kid who jumped a fence to be the first one to the ball. History's being made, and I'm right here with it! Nothing can bring me down, nothing.

Except the shouting that erupts from the kitchen.

I could be across the street in the FBI car and still hear Mom yelling, "You WHAT? YOU SIGNED THE LOYALTY OATH? How could you, Irwin? I thought I knew you."

Whatever my father says in a normal voice makes her madder.

"I will never sign it. Never!"

Mumble, mumble, then even Dad raises his voice, a rare happening. "Look how they fired all those University of California professors for not signing. Brilliant people, Rosalie. They cast them into the wilderness.

We at Hawthorne, we're just small potatoes. It would be easy to jettison us."

"Let them fire me, I don't care. Hear me clearly, Dr. Irwin Rafner, I will never sign. How could I, in good conscience, violate the U.S. Constitution, which is as sacred to me as the Torah? How could *you*?"

I turn the radio up again, to drown them out. Some voice is chirping, "Fresh up with 7-Up!" I yank the cord out of the wall and bury my face in my pillow.

You can be sure the Mick won't be blubbering into his pillow tonight. He'll be out with Lopat and Berra and Rizzuto before he staggers home to Mickey Mantle, Junior.

Must have fallen asleep. The moon's high when I wake up to kick off my sneakers and crawl under the blanket. My first thought: a 565 foot tape-measure homer. But then that thought is bumped by another one that streams along the border of my mind, like a subtitle on one of those boring foreign movies: Life as you've known it is *pfft*.

CHAPTER 7
SUNDAY, APRIL 19

Sure, I know all the stats and juicy news about Big League baseball. Like, who else follows the Class A Colorado Springs Sky Sox, since they're an affiliate of the White Sox? Nobody but me. Yeah, so, knowing baseball and playing it? Two different kettles of fish.

In centerfield, which is the Mick's position, I'm not what you call hot, but I'm not a total wimp, either. Every so often I get under a fly, and I've got a decent arm to toss to Second and Third. Once I even hurled the ball to the catcher and threw a guy out at Home. But Coach Earlywine likes that *thonk-crack* sound when the bat slams the ball. Whenever I come up to bat, the sound you hear is the whoosh of my swing-and-a-miss.

Connor doesn't say much to me at practice, while Coach is driving us into the ground like our spiked cleats. When Coach calls five minutes for water ("just to restore your electrolytes, not to give you pansies a breather"), Connor hangs out with the first baseman, Larry Jukes.

Walking home, Connor and I are stretching for neutral topics.

He says, "You hear that Luke Everly's back from Korea?"

"No kidding? Must've snuck in when nobody was looking."

"Except the G-men."

Whoa, that's not safe territory. Though it's true. Most of the time they sit there spooking everybody who comes to Amy Lynn's or my door. They scribble down license plates and notes about Mrs. Blaire's weekly deliveries, when the only thing *red* about her stuff is the juice dripping from the raspberries that grow wild on her farm. Other times, they wait to pounce like blood-sucking vampires. This morning I caught one holding a milk bottle up to the sun, like maybe the milkman passes us pinko commie propaganda directly from the cows.

It's like those guys live for the time the Sonfelters and Rafners start overthrowing the U.S. government. Like they're actually disappointed at the end of each day when the White House is still standing, and Ike can say with a big yawn, "Nothing happened today, Mamie, girl. Let's hit the sack."

I shift my sweaty glove from one underarm to the other, trying to think of something to break the weird silence. Man, in a minute I'll be whistling something from the Hit Parade. In the good old days, we could spend all day, all summer, talking baseball cards and comparing stats on our favorite players.

Between little bursts of strained conversation, I remember a night last summer at his house. His father and mother were upstairs watching *The Ted Mack Amateur Hour*, and Connor and I were bellied out on the rumpus room floor. On the radio, Tommy Edwards warbled a sappy love song: *Many a tear has to fall, but it's all in the game . . .*

"Yeah, same with baseball," Connor said.

We spread our Fleer baseball cards out in front of us. Each package promised "Funnies, fortunes, facts on every wrapper," plus ten cards and a thin sheet of pink Dubble Bubble you'd snap off in jagged pieces.

I asked, "Get anybody good?"

"Stan Musial, but I already had him. You?"

"Nah, same old stuff. Only Yankee is Phil Rizzuto, but at least he was MVP in '51."

Connor said, "Batting .320 in the Series against the Giants? They wouldn't dare pick anybody else."

"Oh yeah? What about Ted Williams in '41? He was hitting .406, and Joltin' Joe beat him out for MVP anyway."

"Joe DiMaggio, that guy had it over every guy, every game."

I thumbed through my cards, feeling that familiar *ping* when I didn't get a Mantle. A package of Fleers without the Mick was like a PB&J without the peanut butter. Sweet, but nothing to sink your teeth into.

"Another dime down the drain," we said together, like we always did when a new pack of Fleers was old news.

Conner snaps me back to the present. "Heard Luke's pretty shot up, gimpy and kind of wacked out in the head."

"Seriously?" What if he can't stand up on his own two feet, or he doesn't recognize any of us? More than a year since he left. He's never even met his daughter, who's almost walking. She could be walking better than he is. I wonder if he'll be able to shoot baskets, or fix everybody's busted appliances, or cut keys, or any of the stuff he's always been good at. "Think he feels like a hero?"

"Sure should." End of conversation.

On our way to Oxbow Road, we pass through the shopping street for the College. It's called Hollyhock Hill, though it's as flat as western Kansas. It got that senseless name fifty years ago, when they built the clock tower on campus. I hear that when you're standing at the top of Whittier Tower and looking down over Palmetto, the Hill sort of pops up a foot higher than most of the town. I've got to check that out for myself someday.

The Hill is swarming with Hawthorne students—guys in pressed slacks and girls in big swishy skirts, their books clutched to their chests like somebody's out to steal them.

"War of the Worlds" is playing at the Rialto, billed as "The mighty combination of entertainment and electronics that makes motion picture history."

Connor reads the marquee in his best Walter

Cronkite voice: "'From limitless space . . . they're reaching for YOU!'" He starts to grab my arm, then pulls his hand back. We keep walking.

Big relief to finally reach our corner and the familiar rows of two-story College houses, each with its own square of new spring grass and a double-garage door painted the same pukey pastel color as the house. One block to the east, and one block to the west, the houses look just like ours, which is comforting because lately I'm glad to find any evidence of normal life.

Whoa. Connor's house has a huge American flag dipping toward the cement, long enough to mop the driveway and so new that you can still see the fold creases. "You trying to impress the feds, Connor?"

"Old Glory," he says with a laugh.

Amy Lynn comes up behind us. "Urgent business. I'm spitting mad!" She's clearly hoping her poison look will convince Connor to peel off, but he doesn't.

"The girl's seeing red," he says. "There's a lot of that going around."

Amy Lynn takes the bait. "I might as well be a bull with a matador waving the red cape in front of my eyes. I am so mad I could gore somebody."

I jump aside. "Olé."

Connor acts bored.

"It's about what they're doing to my father."

I don't want to hear more. I'm still stuffed from Dad's last lectures. And I don't want Connor to hear it, but she's Amy Lynn, and hey, aren't we all seeing red? "Yeah, fire away."

"I found out why they're after him."

Now Connor's interested. "Yeah? Why?"

Amy Lynn yanks up her white bobby sox. "Because McCarthy has this nutty notion that any veteran of the Spanish Civil War is a communist. Ever heard of anything so preposterous?"

"I've never even heard of the Spanish Civil War. Have you, Connor?"

"Nope."

"Well, that's because you're a grade behind me."

That stings, but I listen.

"Truthfully," Amy Lynn whispers to me, so Connor can't pick it up on his radar, "I just heard of it this morning." Then louder, "It's about the Spanish Republicans against the fascists, back in the thirties."

"Where?" Connor asks.

"You wormbrain. Wouldn't it be dumb to have the Spanish Civil War in, say, Antarctica?"

It would be dumb to have anything except penguins and frostbite in Antarctica, I'm thinking, but also that I'd better keep my mouth shut before I look like a cretin.

" . . . So lots of soldiers from around the world went to Spain to fight with the loyalists. On the side of freedom, of course. The right side, which was kind of the left, I mean if you look at it politically."

"Yeah, the commies," says Connor.

Amy Lynn has her back to Connor, and she rushes through a lot of other stuff, which I translate into something I'm savvy to. It's the bottom of the ninth, Spanish Republicans in the outfield, fascists up at bat. Bases are loaded when some bullfighter of a guy winds up for a spitball pitch right over the plate, and bam! Fascists strike out! Game's over. Fans go wild. Olé!

"My father was one of them, part of the Abraham Lincoln Brigade of American soldiers."

"Figures," Connor mutters.

But I'm wowed. Dr. Sonfelter? The drippy guy with the horn-rimmed glasses and the slide rule sticking out of his pocket? Charging at the bad guys! And now the College is canning this war hero?

"You're just as shocked as I am, Marty. So, McCarthy's saying that all the Abraham Lincoln Brigade men were communists just because they fought the fascists. They weren't, though, they were freedom fighters. The whole thing, totally ridiculous. Tell me you think so."

"I think so." Truth is, I don't know what to think, and now Connor's ducked under the American flag and into the open jaws of his garage, probably to spread the word on Dr. Sonfelter's glorious past. I feel like I'm in a tug of war, with Connor tugging at my right arm, and Amy Lynn dragging me left. The game is to see how far one guy can stretch before he ends up with an empty sleeve flapping in the breeze.

CHAPTER 8
TUESDAY, APRIL 21

Diabolical geniuses that they are, the school honchos decide that we need another air raid drill to keep alert. We gotta be prepared for when the Russians drop the bomb on us. Sixth period, just when I'm thinking, hallelujah, pre-algebra's in my rearview mirror for another twenty-three hours, a siren starts an ear-splitting wail. Miss Camden points to the corny poster on the wall—Bert the Turtle, who knows just what to do when the A-bomb explodes in our schoolyard, which is to pull into his shell. That would save him, all right.

So I'm smashed under my desk inhaling chalk dust on the floor. Bet they don't do the Bert the Turtle thing at the College. They take flying building chunks and oozing radiation like real men.

As if the A-bomb isn't scary enough, everybody's freaked out about polio. *Infantile paralysis.* Brrr, just the name freezes my bones. Yesterday Amy Lynn said, "I'd rather die than be flat on my back in an iron lung all the rest of my life." And that reminds me of Connor saying he'd rather be dead than red. So now, I have four choices: bombed out, dead, red, or locked into one of those giant metal tubes that breathes for me, and the only thing outside the iron lung is my head looking at double mirrors so I can read a book propped up behind me. How the heck do you turn the page?

No contest: I'd rather be red.

Which might explain why Connor's started ditching me at school.

I walk home by myself and hole up in my room. It's my thirteenth birthday, the year of my bar mitzvah, and nobody remembers, not even the parents, who were *there* when I came screaming into the world. They don't worry about stuff like polio or pinko propaganda. They worry about the school desegregation thing in Topeka that the Supreme Court is dragging its feet on, and whether peasants in Mongolia have enough rice in their bowls, and can the Rosenbergs escape the electric chair in, yikes, fifty-eight days? Plus, they're too busy with the hot battle over who's more disloyal, the loyalty oath signers or the stubborn refusers.

Happy birthday to me.

I'm feeling so sorry for myself that I get down my old Mickey Mantle memos. Right, I didn't have the guts to burn them and dissolve the ashes in Clorox.

DATE: October 5, 1951

TO: Mickey Mantle

First Series ever televised, Yankees and Giants. Man, I saw it happen, fifth inning, Game 2. Mays leads off for the Giants and pops a fly to center. You and DiMaggio both run for it. He's old. He shoulda let you have it, but I guess he got greedy in his last Series, and next thing I see is you decked out. What happened out there? Did you trip over your own big feet? Don't feel bad. I do that a lot, 'cause my feet are growing faster than the rest of me. I'm betting you didn't trip. Here's my theory. You saw the Yankee Clipper sailing full speed ahead under that ball, and you slammed on your brakes. Man, I thought you died out there when they carried you off on a stretcher, but I heard on the radio a minute ago that it's only a torn knee. I'm breathing a lot easier now, in case you were worried.

Your friend,
MARTY

If only things were that terrific two seasons later. Last week I heard Mickey say on the radio, "I'll play baseball for the Army or fight for it, whatever they want me to do."

Well, they're turning Mantle down flat because of that bum knee. Here's the kicker, though. The army took the Giants' star rookie from that '51 season—Willie Mays, who popped the fly that ended up tearing Mantle's knee ligaments. Guess Mays got what was coming to him.

Boy, am I ever in a crummy brussels-sprouts-and-beets mood.

There's a loud knock on my door, followed by an even louder, higher one.

"Yeah, what?" I mutter.

Mom and Dad burst into my room full of smiles. Seems the Rocky Marciano and Jersey Joe Walcott of Oxbow Road have called a truce in honor of my birthday.

Mom yanks me off my bed and smothers me with wet kisses. "Did you think we'd forget about your thirteenth birthday, Marty? Not a chance in the world." Dad reaches across her to pat my back and says, "I've made a dinner reservation at the Peach Tree in Newton for the four of us."

Four? Including Amy Lynn?

Mom pinches my arm, but not hard. "Get dressed. Connor will be here in fifteen minutes."

Connor. Aw, man.

CHAPTER 9
TUESDAY, APRIL 21

On the way to my birthday dinner, Connor and I are in the backseat, hunched against the doors. Any farther apart, and one of us would be in the gutter. We're gazing out our windows, not talking. My parents are in the front seat, concentrating on not fighting during this one-night ceasefire. This should be one merry ole birthday celebration. I might have to drown myself in the pool of butter that defines the Peach Tree's famous mashed spuds and softball-sized biscuits.

At the table we try to be party creatures, wisecracking, laughing too loud, and making fun of the family next to us with twin brats in highchairs tossing soda crackers at each other. The two highchairs remind me of twin electric chairs. I don't mention this. I don't want to spoil the fake fun.

Mom teases, "We thought of inviting Mr. Sokolov to the birthday celebration."

He's my bar mitzvah tutor, about as much fun as a paper cut. But we don't have a rabbi in town, and

Wichita's two hours away, so Mr. Sokolov slogs the few Jews in Palmetto through the bar mitzvah year, mostly by phone.

I call everybody into a huddle. "You have to promise no waiters will sing 'Happy Birthday' like they did last year. Swear it?"

Mom flashes a smile. "I don't take loyalty oaths, remember?"

"No waiters will sing," Dad promises, which is scary, because what *isn't* he telling me?

Soon enough, I find out. When the last pieces of chicken are reduced to a graveyard of clean bones, a troop marches out of the kitchen, led by a guy in one of those floppy chef hats, carrying a strawberry shortcake with sizzling Fourth of July sparklers stuck in it.

The waiters don't sing; they just clap in rhythm, and everybody else in the restaurant sings. If I slide under the table maybe they'll think it's Connor's birthday. But now Mom is piling presents and cards around my plate.

After dinner, Dad says, "I'm sure you boys would like some time to celebrate without us old folks around. How about we drop you off by the College and you can go adventuring from there?"

Panic strikes. Connor looks as terrified as I am when Dad leaves the two of us on campus.

"What'll we do now, Con? Wanna just walk home?"

"We're here. Might as well make the most of it."
Like saying *We're out on the highway—we might as well*

let a semi roll over us. "Hey, I know the coolest place on campus."

"Yeah, where?"

"The clock tower. Wouldn't it be *really* cool to climb up to the top of Whittier Tower?"

Wherever you are on campus, you can't miss Whittier Tower poking up at the sky. It says *Hawthorne College* loud and clear. "Sure, but it's locked."

"Wanna bet?" Connor pulls a key out of his back pocket. "What's the use of my dad being in charge of buildings and grounds if I can't smuggle a key out of his locker? I made you a copy yesterday when I was in Newton getting my braces tightened. Happy birthday, buddy."

We sprint across campus like wolves are lapping at our butts. I unlock the creaky door. Start running up the steep, winding steps. Connor huffs and puffs behind me. At about fifty I slow down. Heavy breathing surprises me. I thought I was in better shape than this.

The last couple dozen steps we're sweating out, on our hands and knees, but we keep going up, up, up, until we roll onto the top platform. Connor's ready to beach out on the cool cement, but I warn, "If you don't get off your keister, I'll give you a push. I betcha it's roughly three hundred feet to the ground." I look over the ledge and chuckle. "Your sadly mangled body will make a giant crater."

Sure, a million years from now, people will stand around admiring the fossilized remains of Connor

Dugan, like we did at the La Brea Tar Pits in California two summers ago, the Mick's rookie season.

Want to know what's beautiful? A three-sixty view of Palmetto, where some smart city planner made a law that all roofs had to be red, and God made sure all trees were a dazzling green in the spring. And talk about cool: there aren't any windows at the top, so we've got a terrific fresh breeze whooshing through the clock tower.

And the Hill, yeah, it's a bump higher than the rest of Palmetto.

We ride the wall of the tower like it's a pony, one leg flipped over the side, our backs against a post. No talking, but the silence doesn't feel as freaky as it's been down there on the ground. I finger the key in my pocket. Man, it's like the key to my own kingdom. Hey, it's my birthday. From up here, I'm in charge of the whole world.

Can the emperor of the universe stop an execution fifty-eight days from now?

CHAPTER 10
SATURDAY, APRIL 25

The window's open, but there's no wind. The only thing blowing in our living room is Connor's bugle. Turns out my birthday on Whittier Tower didn't work magic, or at least the magic didn't last for Connor and me as friends. But we've got what my dad calls a Responsibility with a capital R. Ever since Connor's dad got the building and grounds job for the College, we'd wrangled the honor of blowing our bugles at commencement. Since Hawthorne's a Quaker school, it does this Silent Reflection thing during graduation. Connor and I aren't what you'd call natural musicians, so we always have to practice months before, but on the big day, our lungs always pump out those bluesy notes like pros, almost.

Last June, before the FBI, was our best year ever. From the top of Hollyhock Hill, we looked down over the amphitheater in the woods, and what we saw were about three hundred black squares squiggling around, flinging graduation cap tassels. Dean Fennel's amplified voice boomeranged off Trowbridge Peak to the Hill and back. From a distance, say as far away as Wichita, the two hills look like a pair of giant rabbit ears poking up over the Midwestern flatlands.

I crouched back in the grass and whispered, "Battle stations. As soon as Fennel sits down, we're on our countdown. Rockets ready for launch?"

Connor licked his lips and polished his brassy horn on his shirt.

Strung as tight as guitar strings, we waited for the big moment. My eyes followed the second-hand creeping slowly around on my watch. Countdown: four minutes, three minutes, two. I wet my whistle with a swig of water from my Captain Marvel thermos, and stretched my lips with a finger hooked into my cheek. "On your mark . . . get set . . . blow!"

Two majestic, perfectly synchronized trills of our bugles blasted the end of Silent Reflection.

This year it's going to be a lot harder since, you could say, Connor and I aren't exactly synchronized. We nervously toot our horns and stare at the television instead of looking at each other.

Connor's ghoulish in the dark room with the flickering black-and-white images bouncing off his moon face. The TV cuts to a commercial for Kraft Deluxe cheese slices, and we blot it out with a really sour, uncoordinated ditty on our bugles.

From the kitchen Mom yells, "Stop slaughtering cats in there."

By the next commercial (*Ipana Toothpaste keeps your whole mouth cleaner, sweet, sparkling!*) you can at least tell that we're trying to play "Reveille."

Connor wipes spit off his horn. "Okay, we're ready for the big show. Let's go over and tell Luke."

Makes my gut flip-flop. Crossing the street over to the Everlys', Connor gives the FBI guys a stage bow. Dimple Chin ducks his head down, probably talking into the two-way radio to tell bossman J. Edgar, "Start a record on this kid, Connor Dugan."

Luke's sitting on a lawn chair outside his garage, wearing dungarees and a white T-shirt. From my house across the street it looked like maybe he was fixing a radio on his lap, but as we get closer, we see that he's only holding it at arm's length on his knees, staring up to the sky.

He drags his dead eyes down like they weigh fifty pounds each.

Connor and I stand around like idiots, flashing looks back and forth.

Dead air. Suddenly Luke's eyes snap into focus. "Don't . . . blow . . . those bugles."

"Yeah, we're pretty bad," I agree. "We'll never make it to *The Ted Mack Amateur Hour.*"

"No . . . bugles." He turns up to the sky again. I look up. No clouds, no spectacular sunset, not even a crow flying by. What does he find so hypnotizing up there? I look over at Connor, who shrugs me a *what's with HIM?*

He mumbles something about "Sundown, time to roll in Old Glory," and we slink away to our own houses.

Here's the weird thing that makes no sense. Luke was over in Korea fighting communism, but look where it got him. Nowhere. He's locked up in a prison just like the Rosenbergs are, only his prison walls are his own messed-up mind. No fifty-four days to doomsday, because there's no end in sight. That's gotta be way worse.

CHAPTER 11
SUNDAY, APRIL 26

Maybe Luke needs to take up the bugle himself for a few kicks, or play checkers, or go to see a show at the Rialto. Not *War of the Worlds*. Maybe a Dean Martin and Jerry Lewis movie like *The Caddy*. They say it's full of merry mix-ups and fix-ups.

Instead, he sits outside in that lawn chair from sunrise to sunset every day, even in the rain. Just scrapes his chair across the cement a few inches north or south, to keep out of the sun. Sometimes he gets up and limps around the maple tree in his front yard, or picks a few weeds, or scratches Bix, their cocker, but mostly he just sits. When Wendy comes home, she has to jump out of the car, open the garage door right behind him, slide back in the driver's seat, and weave her way around him to wedge the car into the garage.

If Carrie manages to knee her way half into his lap, he'll help her up the rest of the way. Then the two of them sit for a while until Carrie finds something better to do. He never does.

Amy Lynn still babysits Carrie after school and on Saturdays, when Wendy's working at the College library. She tells Mom and me, "All I have to do for Luke is take him a baloney sandwich and a Pepsi. Then, when I put Carrie down for a nap, I sit on the grass and read him *The Grapes of Wrath*. I don't know why I bother. He never says anything."

"Yes, but Steinbeck does," Mom says. She twists her thick braid. "My heart goes out to that poor shell-shocked man. Believe me, Marty, if they try to draft you, I'm going down to the army office and dragging you home by the ankles."

Nothing embarrassing about *my* mom.

Mowing Luke's lawn is tricky, because he sits right on the north edge, and I have to cut a half-circle around him. I call out, real cheerful, "Top o' the mornin', Luke," like he used to say to me before Korea. He barely raises an eyebrow, though he does lift his feet so I can get the lawn mower under them. Guess he doesn't want to risk losing any body parts.

Heading south on his lawn, I mentally test great opening lines:

- *Nice dog you got there.* That only works if Bix is sniffing around, and usually the mutt watches the action and barks like a coward from the living room window.

- *So, what's new?* What could be new? The man just sits there counting clouds.
- *I notice you're building up a serious tan, there, Luke.* That'll only draw attention to his pocked face that still has shrapnel stuck in it.

Man, any safe topics? Heading north with the lawn mower, I settle on one. What guy can resist baseball?

"Think the Yankees'll take the pennant? Fifth straight. Nobody's ever done it." I wait a few seconds, swiping my T-shirt across my sweaty forehead. Might as well be talking to a dime-store dummy. So I turn south again—and hear at my back, real slow:

"If . . . Mantle doesn't . . . get . . . hurt again."

I spin around. "Didn't know you were a Mantle fan, Luke."

He shakes his head and drawls flatly, "Phil Riz . . . zu . . . to. All . . . the way."

"Rizzuto? Come on! He's still limping from the gashes he got when that Browns' catcher spiked him at Second." Oops. I'm not supposed to talk about limping or gashes.

I peek at Luke over the lawn mower handle. Should I keep going? Worth a try. "You know what I like about Rizzuto, though? Talk about *short*stop, he's the shortest guy the Yankees ever fielded, five-foot-five."

Luke spins out, "And that's . . . with lifts . . . in his . . . cleats."

Wow, not just words; a joke! We're on a roll. "Did you hear when Casey Stengel first saw him play, he told Rizzuto he was too small? Said, 'Get a shoebox.' I guess Rizzuto showed Stengel. Get a shoebox, hah!"

No response this time. Maybe a little action will help. "Don't short-change us short guys. We can do amazing stuff." I start zooming around cutting a figure eight.

Luke's spaced out again, off in left field. The conversation has sapped all his energy like the air's been let out of his tires. But it still counts as a conversation on the chart I'm gonna start keeping tonight. Well, why not? I keep baseball records, enough to fill a banana crate. Plus, there are all those Mickey Mantle Memos filed in chronological order, and I've got my bowling league records going back to fourth grade, all nice and neat in a ledger book. So, it's not too weird to keep Luke Everly records, is it? I mean, look at it this way. I can't do a thing about Yankees' hits and runs, and I haven't improved my bowling average in three years.

But *maybe* I can get Luke off of dead center. Gives me hope that he said, "Rizzuto, all the way."

CHAPTER 12
MONDAY, APRIL 27

So, it's game time. Because of my sterling performance at the plate, Coach has decided to stop batting me, which means he doesn't have to field me. Ask me what position I play for the Pirates, and I'd have to answer, *center bench*.

Still, I'm praying for action, all suited up in a uniform that never picks up a speck of field mud. It's eleven to three, South Hadley Mustangs, and we're up, when I feel some weird vibrations coming from the other Pirates. They sprint in from the field, and nobody looks my way, even when I pour on the congrats.

"Great hustle out there, men." Nothing. I clear my throat and speak up: "Hey, Larrimer, your catch at third was legendary, tagging that guy out like that."

"Thanks," Larrimer whispers, without looking at me.

The guys are all kidding around, swinging bats two-at-a-time, swigging orange pop, and acting like I'm a blob of protoplasm oozing on the bench. I pinch myself. Am I *here*?

Coach is giving one of his horrible pep talks before our first batter goes up. "Listen, men, don't give me any of that commie crapola like everybody's equal out there on my field. You wimps are bigger and meaner than that runty pack of mongrels out there. Look at 'em. Disreputable bunch of pantywaists."

"Nice talking, Coach," Larry Jukes says. He can get away with smart-mouthing, because he never walks.

Coach always reminds us, "I rather see you dim bulbs strike out than walk. At least you're swinging and not letting yourself get spooked by a ball zooming at your noggin. So, get out there and kill 'em!"

The ump roars, "Batter up!"

Shire's lead-off. Castleman's on deck, with Connor in the hole. Coach trots out to First to talk to the Mustangs' coach, and that's when Bokser comes up to me and spits a wad at my feet. Misses my cleats by a half inch. His spit aim isn't any better than his pitching.

"What gives?" I ask, easing my foot away. "Connor? Larrimer? Anybody home? What's going on?"

Connor focuses real hard on the pool of foaming spit in the dust. "Lay low, Marty, you're cooked."

Suddenly it seems like my butt is plastered to the bench. I can't move an inch, not even wiggle my big toe.

After the game, where they cream us—big news there—Coach makes us all file through the South Hadley line-up shaking hands and saying *good game, good game.* "Sportsmanship, that's what it's all about," he's always telling us. "Makes men out of you."

Sportsmanship? Lying about it being a good game? Glad I didn't have to sign an oath swearing I meant it, because a bunch of uniformed prairie dogs could have given South Hadley more challenge.

Mom thinks Coach Earlywine is the last surviving Neanderthal. Okay, I agree with that, but not with her take on competition. "This wining/losing thing? I don't get it," she said after the first and last game she came to. "Wouldn't both sides be happier and healthier if every game ended in a tie?"

Hey, Mom, baseball is all about winning and losing. Where's her head? So, after the foaming spit, I feel like the biggest loser in the history of the great American pastime. Especially walking my sweaty self home alone after the game.

CHAPTER 13
TUESDAY, APRIL 28

Welcome to the war zone, the Rafner dinner table. Mom and Dad start out in their separate fox holes, eyeing the enemy across the field of a spaghetti casserole and sending up trial flares.

Mom waves a serving spoon like a band leader. "Creamed spinach, Marty?" A green blob splats on my plate like a lagoon creature. "Isn't the suspense killing you, Irwin? It's been two weeks since Julius and Ethel's lawyers filed the third appeal. What's taking the Supreme Court so long?" She drops a mountain of noodles on Dad's plate, which he eyes suspiciously. Probably wonders if he should have a royal taster before he dares to take a bite.

"They're grasping at straws, Rosalie. What are the latest flimsy grounds? Something like 'deliberate use of false testimony by the prosecution.' It will not hold up."

"Have a little faith, Irwin," Mom shoots back, and the battle's on. She lobs the first grenade. "Dean Fennel turned a rare shade of purple talking to me about the loyalty oath debacle this afternoon. He'd better watch his high blood pressure."

Dad's decided the spaghetti's safe to eat, but only after I shovel a forkful in my mouth and don't keel over. He twirls the noodles neatly on the back of a spoon. "You've backed Fennel into a corner, you know."

"Fennel won't suspend me. Every summer I teach the poetry-writing class. It draws students from all over the country; it's our signature summer course."

"You're mistaken if you think you're indispensable, Rosalie. Neither am I." He takes a deep breath which he blows out like a contented stogie smoker. "That's why you should sign, like I did."

"Traitor! Julius never did this to Ethel. You've betrayed me and everything we stand for!"

Dad shoves his plate away. "The Rosenbergs are on Death Row. You and I are still walking around free to make choices. Aren't you slightly overstating your case, Rosalie?"

That's the aggravating thing about Dad. The madder he is, the calmer he gets, and that sends Mom off into orbit with the space cadets.

"I am *not* overstating it! That mealy-mouthed *I-am-a-dyed-in-the-wool-American* document is a travesty! They should use it to wrap fish."

In fact, the spaghetti is turning to worms in my stomach, plenty enough to catch a big mess of catfish. Wish I were fishing right now. Shadow Lake. Connor and me chewing beef jerky and waiting for a tug on the line, like old times.

"I refuse to sign that statement, no matter how watered-down Sam Fennel makes it look. Demanding loyalty oaths is unconstitutional, un-American, anti-academic freedom—"

"It's necessary if we want to keep our jobs. There's a high-stakes game going on, and Dean Fennel has all the cards."

Spaghetti's hanging from my lips. I'm reeling and sucking it into my mouth at record speeds.

"A game, Irwin? This is no game. We're talking *principle* here. All ideas and beliefs are tolerated in a free country, remember? We shouldn't have to prove that we're loyal. I never would have believed you'd sell out so cheaply."

"We out of grated cheese?" I rattle the green Kraft can dramatically to derail this train, but it keeps speeding along the track.

"I did what I had to do, Rosalie."

"As will I." Mom turns into a stone wall. You can't scale it, and you can't get around it.

He's furious. I can tell by those indentations at the side of his head, which are beating like small drums. He swallows a mouthful of nothing but spit and takes a sip of water while Mom radiates ice vapors across the table.

Finally Dad fires back, "How long do you think those FBI agents are going to let things ride before they strike? They *will* strike, Rosalie. We're living on borrowed time here."

I ball up my napkin and toss it across the table. "I am getting acid indigestion and an ulcer and a goiter."

"Then leave the table," Dad snaps.

You think the Rosenbergs yell at each other in the letters they exchange?

You're never there for me, Julius!

There for you? I'm locked up at the other end of the prison, for God's sake. How there can I be?

You're always busy with your insect collection; no time for me wasting away in this cell.

Time's what I have an endless amount of, Ethel.

Until June 18. Fifty-one days from now.

That should settle the argument.

Suddenly I realize the whole house has gone deadly silent. Even the wheezy fridge seems to be holding its breath. But I've got to get to a game across town in— what?—forty minutes.

My parents are now robots, switched off, frozen in place, and I'm sure not going to beg Connor for a ride to the game. Who's left? Amy Lynn. She has her learner's permit, she'll jump at an excuse to drive.

"Sure," she says. "My parents are at a psychologist appointment on campus. Car's in the garage. I'll take you," she says, her blue eyes gleaming fiendishly.

Big mistake.

CHAPTER 14
TUESDAY, APRIL 28

Amy Lynn handles her parents' big Buick like a maniac. She went forty backing out of the garage without even glancing in the rearview. She slams on the brakes halfway into an intersection where an old lady's crossing. If she'd stepped off the curb a second earlier, that lady would be flat as a sheet pressed through the wringer.

The light changes, and Amy Lynn strips the gears and slams her bare foot on the gas pedal. My forehead hits the windshield. Might not live to warm the bench tonight.

She says, "Do you realize how bad off Luke Everly is?"

"Kind of zombied," I answer, clutching the dashboard. "You oughta drive and not talk."

"Worse than zombied. You can't get two words out of him."

"I did. We talked baseball. He's a Phil Rizzuto fan." True, I haven't heard him say anything since that day, but . . .

Amy Lynn runs a red light, and I shriek.

"What? WHAT? Oh, don't panic. There wasn't anyone else at the intersection." She leans toward me. "It's so, so sad. Everything is, right now."

"You're telling me. Especially if I don't survive this car ride. Keep your eyes on the road!"

"Oh, calm down. Listen, I can't wait for you. Can you get a ride home?"

"No problem." So, I'll be walking home alone again. Pitiful.

◊

I'm getting to be a pro at shining the bench. Two more games, and I'll wear out the seat of my pants and get splinters on my sorry butt. The game's humiliating to watch. Castleman's asleep at second when Shire lobs him an easy one. Larrimer drops his glove, then trips over it and eats dirt. Next minute, Bokser pitches a meatball, and the Newton batter slugs it for a homer—with the bases loaded. The whole game, Coach is howling like a deranged wolf. He should have put me in. I missed out on playing in the most embarrassing game of the season, one you'd tell your grandchildren about some spring training day.

After the disaster's over, Coach mutters, "All you dim bulbs pick up your gear and pile your sorry BEE-hinds into my truck. I'll take you to Wee Wiley's for a root beer and a slice of coconut cream. Just the guys who saw action in this pathetic game."

I'm the only one who didn't see action.

The guys slide around me while they pack up the bases and the chalk-marking machine, the ice chest and the bat bags, and toss all of it into the bed of the pickup. Coach starts to climb up into the driver's seat when he spots me sitting there alone, smashed onto the center of the bench. Comes over and says, "What's your plan, Rafner?"

My mouth is dry; I can hardly push the words out: "Whaddaya mean, Coach?"

"We got six more games before school lets out, and it looks like it's not working out with you and the other Pirates. Ya see that, don't you?"

Now the words are coming faster than I can stop them: "Oh, yeah, I see it. I see that you're all a bunch of scumbags. Sportsmanship, oh yeah. *Kill 'em*, you bet!"

I fall right into his bear trap, and now he snaps it shut. "Maybe it's okay-dandy in your house to mouth off that way. Maybe communists talk to each like that because everybody's pinko-*equal*. But me, I don't take that lip, son. You're off the team, starting yesterday." He hitches up his pants and swaggers over to the truck.

It's a long, lonely walk home. When I get to Oxbow Road, I slink past Amy Lynn's house, hoping she won't see me looking like a sad old popped balloon. I plod up the block so slowly that the FBI guys back up the Studebaker and crawl along with me to watch me more closely. Like I could be passing commie propaganda to the sewer rats.

I ignore them. I've learned to act like the black car is a dead tree stump nobody's chainsawed yet.

Wonder what Mickey Mantle would think of me now. He'd lose all respect for me. Not that he ever had any. If anything ever called for a memo, this does.

From the desk of
IRWIN RAFNER, Ph.D.'s son Marty

DATE: April 28, 1953

TO: Mickey Mantle

Hey, Mick, I know how you felt when they sent you down to the Minors, only worse. Coach kicked me off the Pirates because—get this—he thinks I'm a commie menace. I'm no commie, I'm a centerfielder, like you. After the game, all the guys piled in Coach's pick-up and drove off. Just left me breathing their dust. Let me tell you, it still stung. No, it stunk. Stunk worse than a backed-up toilet.

Your miserable friend,
MARTY (The Red Menace)

CHAPTER 15
WEDNESDAY, APRIL 29

Mom's holed up in her office, which is the phone-
booth size closet under the hall stairs, and she's
pounding out some oddball poem on a typewriter. Some
of it's handwritten in Chinese, because she spent a year
in Kaifeng. Man, her poetry doesn't even rhyme in English, let alone Chinese.

In the living room I'm jiggling the rabbit ears on top
of the TV to shake off the snowy interference on the
screen. Nothing good's on at nine-thirty in the morning, so I might as well work up some spit for the bugle.
Commencement's a few weeks off, and I keep forgetting
to practice.

The doorbell rings. It's a loud clang, like somebody's leaning on the button. I open the door to two
FBI guys dripping rain on their shoes. If I slam the
door, they'll vanish. Ten minutes later, it'll be just be
a cloud of vapor on the porch, and the car across the
street will be gone.

No such luck. The taller guy says, "Special Agent

Milgrim. This is Agent Kluski. Here to speak to your mother, son."

Mom pokes her head out, spots the dark suits and hats, and pounds her fist on the typewriter. All the keys jam together with a sick slurky sound. She comes to the door.

"Yes?"

"Are you Mrs. Rafner?" What, he doesn't recognize her, after hunkering outside our house watching every step she's taken for the past month? Sheesh, he followed her to the dentist last week and sat in the waiting room during her root canal.

"That is I." Normal people don't talk that way; just Shakespeare and Rosalie, when she's acting stuck up.

"Can we ask you a few questions, ma'am?"

"You *can*, but you *may* not." More snotty talk.

"Mind if we step in?" asks Dimple Chin—Kluski—shaking off his umbrella.

"I do, yes. I can't stop you. You've got all the clout."

Can they haul her off to jail for rudeness? She steps back, and the guys slither into our front hall like eels. I turn off the snowy television.

The FBI guys sit, Mom stands, so they both stand up again until Mom drops to the floor with her ankles tucked under her. She's doing a yoga meditation, either to keep her cool or to spook the G-men. It works, both ways. The G-men don't know whether to join her on the rug, or keep standing like dwonks.

"Mrs. Rafner," says Milgrim, "we have some questions about your neighbor."

"Don't tell me, let me guess. You're hounding Theo Sonfelter, right?"

"Well, *hounding*?" Kluski repeats.

I have to hand it to Mom. She sits there with her dress flared out around her, her braid hanging over her shoulder, her arms outstretched, the thumb and middle finger of each hand pressed together.

Milgrim tilts his head toward me. "Martin, could you excuse us for a few minutes?"

Rattles me that he knows my name. But then, why wouldn't he? They've been watching us for weeks. It wouldn't surprise me if they dug up the grave where we buried SnookieCat last summer.

Mom's eyes are still closed, and her throat's vibrating with a faint hum. "My son stays."

Yeah? I want to hang around to see what's going on, but this is what my parents would usually call *adult business*, code for *Get lost, kid*. Mom explains, "I need a witness."

"Your call, Mrs. Rafner." Milgrim plunks his butt in a chair, then barks, "Take a load off," and Kluski drops onto the couch like he's been shot.

Milgrim says, "All right, just a few inquiries, and then we'll be on our way. We'd appreciate your opening your eyes, Mrs. Rafner."

Like she's coming out of a coma, Mom lets her eyes flutter open slowly.

Kluski clears his throat. "Have you noticed anyone suspicious going in or out of the Sonfelter domicile?"

Mom fakes this sweet (killer) look and says in the gentlest (killer) voice, "Gentlemen, I am an English professor at Hawthorne College, a poet, a wife, and the mother of this supreme son. I have neither the time nor the inclination to observe who goes in or out of my neighbors' houses. You're paid to do that, not I."

So then Milgrim gets a little tougher. "To your knowledge, does Dr. Theodore Sonfelter or any member of his family have an association with persons known to advocate the overthrow of the United States government?"

The guys stare down at Mom on the floor, and I start to fidget. I've got an urge to bite my nails, which I haven't done since one got infected in third grade.

"To my knowledge," Mom begins, so calmly that you can hear the air thrumming, "Theo Sonfelter has a constitutional right to associate with whomever he pleases, and I have no idea who or what pleases the man other than arcane mathematical formulae. I suggest you double-check the Bill of Rights, which you're trampling."

Milgrim fires off the next question: "Is he a communist?"

"I couldn't say."

"Are you a communist?"

"I wouldn't say."

Whoa, *wouldn't* say? I don't like the sound of that. Does it mean she *is* a communist but won't admit it? My mom? Man, that's a game-changer that would plunk us in hot water.

Milgrim asks, "Have you ever read a book called *Salt of the Earth*?"

Mom motions around the room, which is rimmed in messy book shelves like every other room in our house. "I have read approximately sixty thousand books."

"Ri-i-ght." Kluski says it like the more books you read, the more suspicious you look. "Have you or any members of your household ever attended a Pete Seeger concert? A Paul Robeson concert? A Weavers concert?"

"Ah, has the government now outlawed popular music? We should have been notified out here in the hinterlands of Kansas." Mom rolls her eyes like Amy Lynn does. Makes me wish I'd known my mother when she was fourteen.

Kluski spins his hat on his finger. "A friend of yours, Mrs. Rafner—we're not at liberty to say who— mentioned that you attended meetings of the American League for Peace and Democracy while you were a student at Stanford, is that correct?"

Mom rises like a Siamese cat in one smooth upward curl, puts on a frosty smile, and says, "I appreciate your stopping by when you have such pressing government business to attend to."

She gives the guys a sweeping bow that ends with a motion toward the front door. "Good day, gentlemen."

"Well, we thank you for your indulgence, and you can be sure we'll be in touch."

I whoosh out a deep breath of relief when they're out in the rain. Didn't even realize I'd been holding my breath. I know it's not true, but I say it anyway: "Guess that's the last we'll hear from *them*!"

Mom sinks into the scruffy recliner, and I notice that her eyes are misted over. She's working her hands like she's soaping them, but they're so dry they whistle.

I kneel beside the chair. "You were terrific, Mom, you didn't tell them anything."

She ruffles my coconut hair. "I didn't have to. They've got bugs all over and know everything about us, Marty. It's just a matter of time until they use it against us."

I'm telling you, it's like a jagged razor drops in my gut. I am sliced.

CHAPTER 16
THURSDAY, APRIL 30

Amy Lynn taps the kitchen door, then bursts in. "Guess what, Marty. I'm a pariah."

"One of those killer fish? I don't get it."

"Everybody at school, even the teachers, think I've been dyed red since my father's under suspicion. Anybody who dares to knock on our door can't miss the FBI spies across the street."

"They've been to my house, too."

But Amy Lynn's so steamed that she doesn't hear. "Becky? Who used to be my best friend? Write her off. Okay, we're at our lockers, and she's peeking into mine, like she expects to see some communist propaganda taped to my back wall. Her shoulders sag when she sees it's a poster of Rock Hudson."

What, no picture of me?

"So, she says, 'Um, I was wondering, Amy Lynn, you planning to stay on the cheerleader squad?' and I tell her, naturally, why wouldn't I? Becky's squirming around and whispers, 'What about other schools?'

"I slam my locker so hard that it flies open again and Rock Hudson falls off the wall. Thing is, she's afraid when we go to Moundridge or Hesston for a game, that they'll think our whole school's turned red. Maybe friends should have to sign loyalty oaths."

Now it dawns on me: *pariah*. It's not a killer fish. It's like when you're the cheese standing alone.

"I'm getting the same cold shoulder from Connor and the other guys on the team." Haven't got the heart to admit to her, or anyone, that I've been kicked off the Pirates.

"It's all so grossly unfair," says Amy Lynn. "I am not one iota political. I couldn't find the Soviet Union on a map if it was painted red and had flashing neon lights all around it! But then, Becky hits me with the blinding truth: 'It's just that, well, suspicion, it's like measles. Nobody wants to catch it from, well, your father. What if he gives the feds my parents' names?' My jaw drops, and I can't even think of a word of response."

By now I'm reaching for the radio. Ever since Mom figured the house is bugged, if we want to discuss anything more important than an episode of *Crusader Rabbit*, we need the hi-fi blaring, or else we huddle in the bathroom where rushing water and flushing toilets muffle our voices.

"And here's the worst part," Amy Lynn says. "My father's lawyer, Mr. Fein? He's coaching Pop for his

HUAC testimony. He actually *is* telling Pop to come up with a list of names—people he can call communists, to give the HUAC more to do and to get himself off the hook. *Off the hook*, what a terrible expression. It sounds like cow carcasses hanging in a meat locker."

"It's what they did to the Rosenbergs," I say, nodding. "Not hanging them in a meat locker, but asking for names, which they wouldn't give, even though Mrs. Rosenberg's own brother testified against her to save his skin and his wife's."

"It's all about loyalty, isn't it? This whole circus."

"And we're the clowns."

Amy Lynn begins washing the tower of dirty dishes (my job) and tosses me the towel while I tell her, "The latest is that the government promised Mrs. Rosenberg that they'd spare her life if she'd offer evidence against her husband. She said no. Said they were both innocent, so she had no evidence to give, even if she'd wanted to."

"Oh, Marty, that is so beautiful. That restores my faith that love triumphs over all."

"Yep." Actually, it made me wonder what I would do to save my own neck. Hey, where did that expression come from? "Which do you think would be worse, Amy Lynn, dying in the electric chair, or hanging?"

"Ga-ROSS, Martin. How do you come up with such stuff?"

Here goes. "Those FBI guys, they came to our house and threatened my mom."

This time she heard it. "They didn't!"

"Yep. And they're asking a bunch of questions. I haven't told anyone but it *feels* like everyone knows, you know? Neighbors, teachers, even the guys on the baseball team."

Amy Lynn links her soap-sudsy pinky through mine. Almost like holding a human hand. "Let's face it, Martin Rafner, our parents are ruining our lives."

◊

Mr. Sokolov, my bar mitzvah tutor, is visiting. He unsnaps his leather briefcase and takes out a twenty-pounder, a book that's got gold pages and fancy red and gold and blue curlicues in the margins. Hebrew on the right column, English on the left. He points to the heading on the page: "Read."

"*Vayera*. Hey, that's my Torah portion!" Amazing, I recognize it.

"Excellent. Read."

I've figured out that Mr. Sokolov loves a good, juicy discussion, and if I get him going, we'll use up the whole hour in English instead my stumbling through the Hebrew. "So, I have a question. Here in Genesis 18, God threatens to destroy Sodom and Gomorrah because people there are evil, right? But Abraham has the guts to wheel and deal with God. Asks, would you spare the place for the sake of fifty innocent people? *Sure, for fifty,*

God says. How about forty? *Yeah, okay, for forty I won't wipe out those two evil cities.* For thirty? . . . And Abraham keeps bargaining with God until they get down to ten innocent people. Sold! Like it's an auction."

Mr. Sokolov gently closes the gold book. "Not exactly, but go on.

"So, doesn't the Lie-Mongering, Red-Baiting Carnivore—"

"Who, Marty?"

"McCarthy."

"Ah." Mr. Sokolov nods.

"He thinks everybody's guilty. Wouldn't you think he'd spare the rest of us for the sake of, say, ten innocent non-commies?"

"I see where you're going with this."

"So?"

"Very clever." Mr. Sokolov smiles and opens the book to *Vayera* again. "Read, please."

No word from Milgrim and Kluski yet. Waiting.

CHAPTER 17
FRIDAY, MAY 1

May. I wonder if Mr. and Mrs. Rosenberg woke up this morning in their cells at opposite ends of Sing Sing and realized that it's going to happen next month. Forty-eight days to doom.

It's not even six-thirty, and there's already steam coming out of Mom's ears. Something to do with the newspaper open on the table.

Mom looks like a raving lunatic this morning. She's undone her braid, and the hair's flying all over in accordion ripples. It's a lot grayer than I thought.

She slides the *Palmetto Sentinel* across the table so I can't miss the letter to the editor that she's boxed in red.

Just as language separates us from animals, it is the freedoms in this country that separate us from the tyrannical Soviet Union. Personally, I find it impossible to understand why a citizen loyal to the United States, if in fact that is what Rosalie Rafner truly is, would not uphold those freedoms by signing a simple declaration of allegiance. Refusal to do so leads a thinking person such as myself to conclude that Professor Rafner has communist leanings. Perhaps the College should inquire further into her background.

—An American Through-and-Through

"Aw, Mom," I groan. This has gone way public. The *newspaper*!

"Not to worry. I've already composed my retort." She hands me a typewritten sheet. "See what you think."

Dear Through-and-Through:

You clearly do not understand the First Amendment. Try having FBI agents outside your door twenty-four hours a day, spying on you, and threatening you and your family, and then maybe you'll understand how easily your rights slide away, one small toehold at a time.

—Rosalie Weitz Rafner, a Person of Principle

She gives me a hug; wiry hairs fly in my mouth. "I know it's been rough, Marty. We'll get through this. Stay with me on it, will you?"

"That's asking a lot, Mom."

"Signing the oath is the first step on the slippery slope, Marty. You understand what your father's overlooked."

That's when Dad comes in, with his glasses buried in his tight curly mop. "I've heard this speech before," he says wearily and pours himself a glass of tomato juice.

Mom hands him the newspaper.

"I read it. It's cold and calculating. But you must understand this, Rosalie. You're clinging to the Bill of Rights as a life preserver. It will fail you. We're going under; we're drowning."

My rye toast is going to pop up in a second, and I'm forcing myself to blot out their voices and focus on the big decision—apricot jam or butter—when I see Mom's shoulders sag. I stand in front of the open fridge, jam jar in one hand, butter dish in the other, as she lets it all hang out.

"I couldn't bring myself to tell you this yesterday, Irwin. Dean Fennel put me on suspension. He gave my poetry class, *my* poetry class, to Ed Harvey, who hasn't written a single lyrical word since World War I."

Gotta give old Irwin credit. He resists saying *I told you so* and actually puts his arms around Mom and lets her beat her fists on his nightshirt.

Butter and jam, both, definitely. I'm way out of my league here.

Or why not cream cheese? I'm tearing through the fridge looking for the silver package, slamming the vegetable bin drawer, knocking over a jar of pickles.

Mom's never this vulnerable, and Dad? He's actually *rocking* her and running his fingers through her loose hair.

This is too weird for me. I slam the refrigerator door and spear the rye out of the toaster.

I'll choke it down dry, then go mow Luke's lawn.

◊

Turns out Luke watches everything up and down the street, though he hardly ever leaves his lawn chair. I'm mowing, and he suddenly stands up and follows me, limping across the front lawn and shouting over the putt-putt of the mower.

"What . . . happened . . . with you and . . . your friend . . . up the . . . street?"

I nearly whack a rose bush, I'm so surprised. I stop pushing the mower and mop sweat off my face with the bottom of my T-shirt. "It's sort of complicated." Yeah, like Connor's steering clear of me, 'cause his family's *different*, not pinko like mine.

Luke nods in that slow-motion way. His heart rate must be down to about twenty beats a minute. Then he says, "It's . . . because of . . . the . . . communist . . . business, right?"

"Yeah, kind of."

He's flicking his way-long finger nails and frowning, with his eyes just dark slits. He's mad.

"Oh, I get it. You think my whole family's soft on communism, and that bugs you 'cause you were over there in Korea fighting the commies and got—messed up."

Luke glares at me, then limps away. His war wounds are probably hurting him in all this soupy humidity. I start pushing the lawn mower again and hear him yell at my back, clear as sunshine, "If that's what you think, kid, nothing I can do about it."

I spin around. His whole sentence is a tease. I want more. But he's already sunk into his chair under the basketball net, with that spacey-spooky look like he's checking out the rings of Saturn with his naked eye.

CHAPTER 18
SATURDAY, MAY 2

A bucket of rocks has landed in my stomach, and they're working their way up my gullet into my throat. By seven o'clock, I feel like I might explode if I don't get some sympathy.

I pick up the phone, hold my breath, swallow gobs of pride, and dial Connor's number. His father answers.

"Connor home?"

"D'jou see the American flag waving outside our house? Tells you something about us that's different from you folks. I can't have my boy hanging around with communists, which'll get my own rear twisting in the wind at the College. So, best you don't call here again. It's nothing personal."

Sure feels personal. You'd think Mr. Dugan would realize that I'm me, and my mother is somebody outside my skin, and just because she refuses to sign that stupid loyalty oath that's gotten us in hot split-pea soup up to our pits, doesn't mean my whole family is plotting to put the White House on a gigantic tractor trailer and move it to Red Square in Moscow.

These thoughts are dragging me down into a black hole. Mom and Dad are both working at the dining room table.

"Hey, can we talk?"

Mom whips around like she's just been kicked. *Can we talk* is usually her phrase. "Sure, Marty, what's on your mind?"

Dad puts down the manuscript he's editing and caps his pen. They both wait for me to speak.

"Maybe it's not the worst thing that's happening to our family with all this—do I dare say the word?—pinko stuff that's going on."

Mom curls her lip.

"Coach kicked me off the team." Saying it out loud makes it feel even worse and final.

"Because of your performance?" Dad asks.

I shake my head.

"Because of me?" Mom clunks the table with a thick Chinese dictionary. "That ignorant, tyrannical Neanderthal has no concept of—" She stops and leans over to put her arms around me. "Oh, Marty, I'm so sorry my stubbornness has hurt you this way."

Is that what the Rosenbergs told Michael and Robby?

Dad reaches for my arm across the table. "You want me to talk to the coach?"

"No! I want all this to stop! It's not just Coach—*everyone* looks at me differently now, including Connor." I swallow back the details. "It's not fair."

Dad sighs deeply. "Rosalie?"

Mom clenches her fists. "I'm sorry about how this is affecting our family. Sorrier than you can ever guess. But I can't back down now. Someday Marty, you'll thank me for being true to my convictions."

Yeah, sure.

Dad doesn't waste a lot of time on sappy sympathy. Just turns on the radio to muffle the sound of our voices. "Martin, I think you should know what's going on with the Sonfelters, in case Amy Lynn hasn't given you the full story. Theo's appearance before the HUAC in D.C. is next week."

"I heard."

"He has some options," Mom says, and Dad looks annoyed that she's butted in. "He can plead the First Amendment, meaning his right to free speech and free association with anybody he pleases."

Dad pushes his glasses up into his hair. "The problem with that is, he could be held in contempt of court."

"Meaning?"

"Maybe a year in prison."

"Sheesh!"

"There's a better option," Mom chimes in. "He can invoke the Fifth Amendment, which is his right not to testify against himself. Husbands and wives can invoke

the Fifth so they don't have to testify against each other."
She glares daggers at Dad.

He dodges the sharp points. "That might have worked a few years ago, but nowadays everyone assumes you're guilty—that is, you're a communist—if you plead the Fifth. He'd be blacklisted, and no other college or industry would hire him."

Mom mutters, "He'll be lucky to get a job bagging groceries."

Pretty grim. "Third option?"

"Well, when they throw him the central question— are you now or have you ever been a member of the Communist Party?—"

Like Milgrim did to Mom.

"—he can state clearly that he isn't and wasn't ever." They exchange looks I can't read. "You might as well know this, Martin. He could be lying."

"He really *is* a communist?" What's that make Amy Lynn? Is it something you inherit, like brown eyes, or do you catch it like the measles? Does she know?

Mom reaches for my hand and roughly rubs my fingers. "Then the HUAC will produce a witness, someone who swears he's been at a meeting with Theo, or someone who fought with him in Spain, or almost anyone who's willing to come forward to save his own hide, and he'll testify that Theo is, in fact, a party member."

"In which case Theo would be convicted of perjury and would go to prison," Dad adds.

"You're telling me he has a fifty-fifty chance of ending up behind bars?"

Mom says, "He'd get one year for contempt with the Fifth, or five years for lying under oath. It doesn't take a Ph.D. to figure out which is the better choice."

"Amy Lynn's father could rot in the slammer for five years?" I keep thinking of Connor saying, *I'd rather be dead than red.* Five years in prison would be like being dead, like living in an iron lung.

"Well, there's still another option," Dad says, "a way for him to get his job back at the College. He'd have to feed the committee names."

Mom jumps to her feet and rips a dead leaf off her avocado plant. "That's like throwing raw meat to sharks. And it would ruin so many other lives."

I ask, "Yeah, but couldn't he give them names of people the committee already knows are communists?"

Dad shakes his head. "The fact is, it doesn't matter who he names. These hearings aren't designed to get at truth. They're designed to intimidate, to strike fear in the hearts—"

"—of patriotic American citizens like us!" Mom shouts.

"Sit down, Rosalie, you're making me nervous."

I'm sinking in my chair, practically at nose level with the table, as if the less of me that's showing means less that can feel crummy about this whole sorry mess.

Sooner or later I'm going to have to come right out

and ask: If Dr. Sonfelter's a communist, and so are the Rosenbergs, Mom and Dad, are *you* communists?

Can you be a patriotic American and a communist at the same time?

Dad lowers his voice to a whisper: "There is one more option. Not a good one, but a possibility." There's a long, dicey pause. "Theo can go underground. Just . . . disappear."

CHAPTER 19
WEDNESDAY, MAY 6

The phone is ringing like crazy. I'm ninety-seven percent sure it's not Connor calling. I snap the phone up on the sixth bounce.

"This the Rafners?" The man's voice is familiar, but I can't place it. It's kind of muffled, like he's trying to disguise it, the way they hold a handkerchief over the mouthpiece in the movies. "Feeling good about all the commies in your house?"

"Sir?" I glub down a huge lump in my throat. "Who is this?"

"A friendly word of advice." He doesn't sound at all friendly. "Pull down the ladder to the attic, the one right over your head."

How does he know we've got an attic ladder in our front hall? And who *is* this guy?

"Get down a steamer trunk and start packing."

My heart's hammering. "We're not going anywhere."

"Sure you are, if you know what's good for you. Julius and Ethel didn't skip the country to Mother Russia fast enough before the feds nabbed 'em. So, my advice? Pack up quick and ride that Red Rail right outta town. Because if you don't, there's plenty of patriotic Americans with loaded shotguns right here in Palmetto who'll be more'n happy to speed you along." Clunk. Dial tone.

"Dad!" I barge into his office, shaking down to my toes.

He's tilted back in the swivel chair behind the desk. The chair squeaks, which makes my teeth feel scritchy.

"Sorry to bother you, Dad. It's this creepy phone call I just got."

"I've been getting them, too, here and at my office on campus."

"Think we should tell the FBI guys across the street?"

"There's no need to," Dad says hoarsely. "They listen in on every call in and out of this house. We're under siege, do you understand?"

Yeah, I understand all right. The anger trickles up my spine and pumps hot loads of understanding into my head. Feels like a noose is tightening around my neck, and the floor's about to drop out from under me, and I wonder again, is hanging any better than electrocution? Did they give the Rosenbergs a choice? My hands are shaking. I ram them in my pockets and beat a path out of Dad's office like my heels are on fire.

Standing here at the window makes me look like a complete drip, but there's Amy Lynn across the street, and she's got her legs propped up the wall of Luke's house. She told me she'd be reading *Mad Magazine* to Luke, to see if she could appeal to his funny bone. If he still has one. Amy Lynn tilts her head back and waves to me over her shoulder. Luke's as still as a department store dummy.

Gotta pull myself away from the window. The radio's blaring an obnoxious commercial for Colgate Chlorophyll Toothpaste, which Mom refuses to buy ever since they started putting chlorophyll in dog food to improve doggie breath.

Yankees against the Indians. Cleveland's third-baseman Al Rosen is the man to watch, if you take your eyes off the Mick for a sec. Man, Rosen is batting .336, which, as Bubbie Sylvia says, "isn't bad for a nice Jewish boy."

The thing about radio is that you see and smell and taste every detail of the game—with your ears. Mel Allen pours it all into mine. No game is complete until some pitcher throws a gopher ball to a Yankee slugger, and Mel Allen yells, *Going, going, gone!*

Now I hear the pre-game roar of the crowd and see thousands of hepped-up fans packed into Yankee Stadium. I suck in the smell of hot peanuts when bags fly past me down the bleacher line. There's the mighty smack of the ball in my glove, because tonight I am the catcher warming up Eddie Lopat, who'll be pitching for New York. I'm telling you, I am *there*, even if I'm invisible to Connor and all the guys on my team. Ex-team.

Mr. Sokolov will be here to listen to me struggle through my lousy Hebrew pronunciation in twenty minutes, so I don't want to miss a single minute of the game till then. But I can't help thinking, *It's only a game, only a game, and there will be lots of other ones.*

Before I can chicken out, I pull the plug, open the back of the Philco, and jerk out a wire. Screw the radio together, pick it up, still warm, and take it across the street.

I don't tell Luke anything directly. I just belly-ache to Amy Lynn, "Stupid radio went out on me, at the worst possible time. Man, I missed the opening pitch. I am so ticked, I'm tossing this piece of junk in the trash."

Amy Lynn rolls over on her stomach as I wrap the cord around the radio with vengeance, choking it to death.

And like magic, Luke says, "Lemme . . . have . . . a . . . look."

He's got it fixed in minutes. You can bet there's gonna be a whopping entry about this in my Luke box scores.

Turns out the Mick went hitless against Cleveland, probably because I wasn't listening. Can't win 'em all.

CHAPTER 20
FRIDAY, MAY 8 –
SATURDAY, MAY 9

Last night it rained flash-flood level, and I thought our windows would crack from the golf-ball-sized hailstones, but they didn't. The Palmetto Pirates game after school tomorrow is gonna be a soggy one. And I'm not gonna be there, not even on the bench, not even in the stands, not even lurking behind a garbage can. I'm stretched out on my bed like a beached whale.

I turn up the radio full blast and bury my head under my pillow.

Mom says we're living under the sword of Damocles. My clever response is, huh? Turns out, Damocles was this Greek guy a couple thousand years ago who had a sword hanging right over his head by nothing but a single hair. Potential severe ouch.

The FBI sword could drop any time, and we'd be chopped meat.

Plus, summer's coming soon, and they're not even opening the city pool this year because of the polio scare. I don't have a single summer plan—no summer baseball league—except busting my butt with Mr. Sokolov drilling for my bar mitzvah in October. I might as well sleep right through the execution in forty-one days.

It's tempting; I'm already lying on my bed. My pre-algebra book's propped up between my gut and my raised knees, and the squiggles are swimming around like ants building one of those thumb-sized cities they're famous for. Man, how can Amy Lynn's father spend his life on this? He'll put the senators on the HUAC committee to sleep with just a page of this stuff.

Just when I'm about to doze off myself, I hear a crash in the living room. When I run out there, I see that somebody's finished what the hail left undone. The window's shattered. Now there's a pile of glass on the floor and a bad chip in our coffee table, caused by a big rock with a note tied around it. I carefully unfold the paper—fingerprints; maybe the G-men will find the guy, unless they're the ones who hurled the rock.

Nah, somebody else. The note says:

THE ONLY GOOD RED
IS A DEAD RED
DDT (DROP DEAD TWICE)

Underneath is a picture of two electric chairs with grinning stick figures in them, with the date *June 18, 1953*.

My heart does cartwheels. Why isn't the FBI chasing

the guy who threw the rock instead of sniffing our milk and pawing our mail?

◊

Dad gets a fix-it man to board up the window until we can get a new one. Good thing, too, because there's another storm the next day. Thunder rumbles, lightning flashes. Rain pelts a drumbeat on the plywood over the window. Mom and Dad and I are sprawled on the couch and chairs in the living room. I'm trying not to doze off while Mom reads us stanzas from her latest collection, *Vainglory*, or maybe it's *Gory Veins*, when the doorbell rings. As heavyweight champ Rocky Marciano might say after pulverizing Joe Louis: *saved by the bell*.

Turns out, we're *doomed* by the bell. It's our old friends, dripping again. Maybe they pick the rainiest days to come in because they're afraid the Studebaker might float to the next county, carrying them someplace without commies to hassle.

Mom's ready to give the G-men some snappy sass, but Dad runs interference, oozing charm. "What can we do for you gentlemen?" He's the guy who can talk to the southern African people who make impossible click sounds down deep in their throats. What's so hard about a couple of professional government spies who know more about us than we know about ourselves and could throw us in the slammer?

"Mrs. Rafner, we'd prefer to speak with you in private," Milgrim says.

She fires back, "No dice. As I said last time, I need witnesses."

"My wife and I are partners," Dad adds. "You may speak freely, because our son is a junior partner in this family enterprise."

Since when? Yeah, I defended the Rosenbergs to Connor. Yeah, more than once I've spit on the FBI car and kicked its tires. But I honestly gotta wonder if it's a good move for me to be a partner in Rafner and Rafner, the maybe-commies.

"Suit yourself." Milgrim might as well add, *It's your funeral.* He crosses his ankles like an old lady, showing white and green argyles. I wouldn't be caught dead in socks like those.

Milgrim, with his notebook balanced on his knees, pokes his chin in Mom's direction. "Mrs. Rafner, our wish is to spare you as much unpleasantry as possible."

Mom sneers. "That's evident." Dad moves across the room to her side, and it's me and the two agents on my side.

I'm thinking of that game we used to play at recess: *Red Rover, Red Rover, send Marty right over.* I'd bombard the other side, ramrod my way in like a raging bull, while the people in the line locked their arms to keep poor little freckle-faced Marty out. You know, one of those cruel games we all loved in grade school.

Milgrim tips his notebook shut by raising one knee. "Ma'am, it is my duty to inform you that you are at risk of deportation."

Mom laughs. "Deportation to where? This is the only country I've ever lived in."

"To Poland, Mrs. Rafner, where you were born in 1909."

"Oh, gentlemen, you've got your facts bass-akwards. I was born in Poland, true, but only because my mother was visiting her parents, and I came four weeks early. Two more weeks, and I'd have seen the sun in New York, not Krakow."

Dad puts his hand on Mom's arm—*Back off*, he's telling her. "Agent Milgrim, my wife is a U.S. citizen by virtue of being the child of citizens, regardless of where she first drew breath."

Milgrim leans forward, ready to pounce, and Kluski throws him a warning look. Good cop/bad cop.

Kluski says, "I regret to inform you, Mrs. Rafner, that neither of your parents completed the citizenship process, and since you were not born on American soil, I'm afraid you aren't a citizen of this country."

The color bleaches from Mom's face. Dad grips her arm; they're a fiercely linked Red Rover chain.

They can do that? Deport her? Man, they can! They're the feds. They can ship my mother back to Poland in the blink of an eye!

CHAPTER 21
SATURDAY, MAY 9

Milgrim isn't done delivering bad news. "We have reason to believe that charges will be brought against you under the Internal Security Act of 1950, commonly known as the McCarran Act. You, a Polish national, are a clear and present danger to the security of the United States."

"Absurd!" Mom cries.

Milgrim opens his notebook with his thumb and index finger like he's picking up a dirty diaper. "You have been a member of two subversive organizations, namely the Congress of American Women and the National Council of the Arts, Sciences, and Professions."

They move closer, as if Mom's going to bolt. Suddenly we've switched from Red Rover to Farmer in the Dell. I'm the cheese, standing alone.

Mom sounds breathless. "The first group merely advocates for equity for women, and the second is a professional fellowship organization. I hardly think—"

Milgrim cuts her off. "Known to be communist fronts, both."

Mom takes a deep breath for her comeback blow. Which doesn't come. Instead, a zap of lightning sends our lights flickering.

Great. We're gonna lose power and crawl around in the dark with these guys to hunt up candles and matches.

There's a quick blackout, but after a second the lights hold. Phew! Our window air conditioner roars in the corner, water dripping from it and pinging onto a tin pan.

Mom asks, "When did democratic ideals of justice and equality become subversive?"

"When they're in the hands of foreign nationals linked with communist front organizations, Mrs. Raffner." Kluski's brilliant comment.

Dad throws Mom a *keep quiet* signal. "What is my wife's status? Her options. Be frank and specific." No more Mr. Nice Guy, ambassador to the world.

Milgrim says, "She'll be called before the SISS. That would be the Senate Internal Security Subcommittee."

"I'm not an infant or an imbecile. Address me directly." Mom's voice is chilly, still shaky.

"As you wish. The second option is that you voluntarily return to your homeland, Poland."

"This is my homeland! My family, my work, my life are all right here. For God's sake, I've voted here for twenty-three years."

"A clerical oversight." Kluski shakes his head sadly.

"If you don't go voluntarily, you'll be arrested and deported forthwith."

Nobody says *forthwith*, not even Mom, who bites her lip until it turns white.

"Hypothetically, what if we relocated to another country?" Dad asks.

Oh, no, he's going to haul us into the African jungle.

"You and your son are free to go, sir. However, your wife will not be issued a passport.

Correction: she'll have a one-way trip to Poland, at which point her passport will be confiscated. I'm truly sorry to tell you this."

"I'll bet." The words zing out of my mouth, which earns me a warning scowl from Dad.

Mom drops into the recliner. "All because I refused to sign an unconstitutional loyalty oath?"

"No, ma'am," Kluski says. "That's only the tip of the iceberg."

"What my partner means is that you're in violation of federal statutes. As a foreign agent, you're required to notify the Immigration and Naturalization Service of your whereabouts annually. Failure to do so makes you an alien living illegally in the United States, in violation of the Immigration Act of 1924. Furthermore, as an enemy alien and member of two communist organizations, you are in violation of the McCarran Act and, pursuant to your membership, you are required to register under the Internal Security Act of 1950."

"Which President Truman vetoed," Mom says.

"But which veto Congress overrode and duly enacted," Milgrim adds snidely.

Dad interrupts this deadly ping-pong match. "And if she signed the loyalty oath now?"

"I'm afraid that wouldn't help, sir, now that her immigration status and communist associations have come to the attention of the Director."

Ah, the fascist, J. Edgar Hoover.

Kluski adds, "And Senator McCarthy, of course."

What a combo on their team, like pitting a National League catcher/pitcher battery against the squirrely Palmetto Pirates.

Milgrim stands up, smoothing his pin-striped slacks. At least we can't see the stupid argyles now. He flips a page in his notebook and acts like he's just noticed a little detail. "By the way, Yossele Mendelev. The name rings a bell?"

I remember Dr. Mendelev. He stayed with us when I was nine. Those nights when my parents didn't have College people over to hang out with him, he challenged me to a game of chess. Truth is, I never liked chess and never got any good at it, but I liked Dr. Mendelev and the story he told me in his thick, creamy Russian accent, a new episode every chess game. Man, it was better than *Tom Corbett, Space Cadet.*

Dad closes his eyes, but Rosalie out-stares Milgrim, who says, "This Mendelev, we understand he boarded with you in 1949, correct?"

Mom bristles. "Dr. Mendelev is a world renowned poet who honored Hawthorne with a one-month residency, and if you say it was 1949, I'll assume you're right."

"World renowned," Milgrim says. "Would that *world* include the Soviet Union, from which he came, and to which he returned in June of 1949?"

Dad announces, "This interview is over, gentlemen."

"Yes, yes, forgive me." Milgrim's nearly groveling. "We'll leave you to consider your options." He jerks his head, and Kluski shoots to his feet like he's got a firecracker up his rear.

"You will be served summons papers, Mrs. Rafner. Your SISS hearing is Wednesday, June third, in New York City." Milgrim advises, "Allowing for the realities of train travel, plan on approximately a week. My colleague and I will leave you to make your decision: voluntary deportation, or testifying at the hearing."

"*If* she's served papers," Dad says.

"*When* she is served. And may I offer a recommendation? Brush up on your notes about Yossele Mendelev. Good day."

He and Kluski prance like stallions to the door and leave us to pick up the lives they've just smashed into atoms.

Nobody has a clue what to say, so we all yammer stupid things.

Mom: "There are fresh sheets on your bed, Marty."

Dad: "Who wants to go out for ice cream?"

Me: "I'll never be able to learn Polish. Even Poles can't pronounce half the words in their language."

We're like the Tower of Babel, until Mom puts two fingers in her mouth and lets out a blood-curdling sailor's whistle. "Irwin, there's a package of Lucky Strikes in the buffet drawer. I need a cigarette."

Bad sign. She hasn't smoked since 1947 when she exhaled into the fishbowl, and Rainbow went belly-up.

Dad comes back with the Lucky Strikes and lights Mom's cig like Humphrey Bogart on the silver screen. She blows satisfied smoke rings out her mouth. "These cigarettes are stale."

Finally we can all let out our breath and start to make some sense of the mess we're in.

Mom waves the cigarette around. "It's a trumped-up case. They're harassing us, trying to intimidate us. My parents both became citizens before I was born. It was their proudest accomplishment. There's a picture that was taken the day they got their citizenship, each of them wearing an Uncle Sam hat and waving an American flag."

"I'll call your mother," Dad offers. "We'll see if she can produce the citizenship documents, or at least the dated photograph. First I'll call Barry Siegel and see how we go about getting a good immigration lawyer."

Mom nods. "We have to let the College know, too."

"Maybe we should cancel my bar mitzvah," I suggest.

"No!" my parents say together, and Dad adds, "We have to keep life as normal as ever."

When was the last time it was normal? Truth is, things haven't been normal since Judge Kaufman's gavel came down in the courtroom the day he sentenced Mr. and Mrs. Rosenberg to death, and that was two years ago. Forty days to go, but who's counting?

Mom backs toward the kitchen. "This situation calls for chocolate chip cookies."

We recognize this strategy and know to stay clear of her path. When Rosalie Rafner's mad, she attacks the kitchen like a crazed army cook. In a minute we hear a bowl spin viciously on the counter. Drawers jerk open, with silverware flying. The fridge slams shut. Two eggs are smacked against the side of the bowl, the empty shells hurled across the room, splat, into the sink.

"I'm going into the combat zone," I offer bravely.

"At your own risk." Dad tosses me a *National Geographic* as a shield. "That's to protect you from airborne cookie dough." He's started making his list, and he heads for the phone.

In the kitchen, Mom's rolling two walnuts across the table.

"Aw, Mom, you're not putting nuts in the cookies, are you?"

"No, I want the sheer pleasure of cracking them." She grabs the walnuts and rolls them in her hand, where they click like dice. "See these two shrunken heads? This one's Milgrim, and this littler one is Kluski." She locks Milgrim in the vise of the nutcracker and coldly smashes him. A curvy smile spreads across her face as she hands me the nutcracker. "Want to take care of Kluski?"

"Ooh, yeah!" I crack him open, and it feels as good as a line drive to centerfield.

CHAPTER 22
FRIDAY, MAY 15

"**F**or heaven's sake, Marty, put that confounded bugle away!" Mom cries. Sheesh, I've only played about three wrong notes . . . out of six. But she's in a funk and not up for a serenade. Why? Partly because the Rosenbergs lost another appeal, probably their last, and their execution date is looming closer. Thirty-four days, now. But the bigger part is that she's scared—we all are—because she's decided to testify if the committee calls her. I would have tried to talk her out of it, but anything's better than sending her (us?) to Poland.

The National Lawyers' Guild has sent over a lawyer and some volunteer law students from Washburn University, over in Topeka, to prepare Mom to testify in front of the SISS. They've set up cots in the attic so they can work around the clock—even brought in a private eye to sweep the place for bugs. There's always somebody thundering up and down the stairs, or peering in our fridge, when they're not arguing up in the attic.

The lawyer, Mr. Quincy, and Vic, the immigration

intern, have different game plans for Mom, and nobody seems to be coaching the series. They argue and work up in the attic, with Dad refereeing.

But everybody agrees Bubbie better find those citizenship papers, and pronto. The Immigration and Naturalization Service has no record of a Sylvia Sandler Weitz or Avrum Weitz becoming naturalized way back in 1907. Mom remembers that picture of Bubbie and Zeyde in the Uncle Sam hats, the day they took the citizenship oath, but maybe her memory is bogus. Maybe Bubbie and Zeyde lied about becoming citizens for so many years that Bubbie believes it really happened.

"More likely the papers have been *disappeared*," Quincy notes.

Mom's spitting mad. "You mean the INS and the FBI are in cahoots against me? They're supposed to be *for* the people, not against."

"Theoretically," Dad says, fanning himself with a sheaf of lawyer papers he's been monitoring. Documents. We're living in the Grand Canyon of documents.

There's lots of talk about whether Mom should read from a prepared statement, or whether she should plead one of the Amendments. Should she battle the committee on the grounds that the entire thing is unconstitutional?

Or should she simply name names?

Mom says, "I will not inform on other people, and that's final."

Mr. Quincy, who doesn't know yet how stubborn my mother is, dares to ask, "Even if the committee already has those names, Rosalie? Even if they're merely asking for confirmation?"

"Not even if the people are six feet under!" Rosalie shouts. "I refuse to implicate anyone else. In the Torah, there's a word for informing on someone. It means eating someone else's flesh. Cogitate on that image, people: eating someone else's flesh. This I will not do."

Who'd expect that Rosalie Rafner would suddenly thump the Bible?

Mom turns to me with a sickly smile. "Check the Yankees schedule, Marty. Maybe we can take in a game while we're in New York."

Mr. Quincy growls and slams his briefcase. He just doesn't appreciate a woman like my mom. Some days, I know how he feels.

◊

So, it's totally insane at my house, but Luke's easy to be with. No demands, no complications, no storm of words or papers. He used to be the crackerjack key grinder in town, and I'll use any excuse to go across the street.

"Hey, can you make a copy of this to hide in the petunias in case I forget my house key, or the FBI needs a surefire way to get inside when we're out?" Always ready to help the U.S. gov.

Luke studies the other key on my chain, the one to Whittier Tower, Connor's birthday present to me. He says hoarsely, "Key's . . . new . . . but . . . real . . . old cut . . . of . . . teeth."

I don't know if I should tell him, but what the heck. He doesn't talk to anybody else, so the secret's safe. "You know that clock tower on campus? Okay, I'm not exactly saying this key unlocks it."

He nods and goes into the house, while I stand there like an idiot. Through the little square of a basement window, I watch the light flash on in his shop, then flicker the way it does when you run a grinding machine like a key-cutter.

In ten minutes, I've got a new house key. I go home and test it: it works like a knife sliding through warm spit.

◊

"Luke made this. Seems like he's coming around." I flash the shiny new key at Amy Lynn, who's sitting on her porch looking like she's just seen that 3-D horror movie, *House of Wax*. In fact, she looks like a wax figure herself.

"Dreamer," she says flatly. "He's not coming around. In fact, Wendy's planning to take Carrie and move back to her parents in Newton, at least for a while until she gets her own place."

"How do *you* know?"

"I overheard her talking to her mother on the phone. She's packing."

I plunk down on the step next to Amy Lynn. "That'll kill him."

Amy Lynn shrugs. "Luke won't even notice."

I don't agree, but I decide it's best to drop the subject. "How's your father's hearing in D.C. going?"

"He's there, but they keep postponing it." She answers sharply, then turns away from me.

Something's up. I don't want to bug her. Guess she'll spill it when she's ready. I'm not telling her the whole story yet, either.

Before the day's out, two weird things happen. First, there's a guy at our door with his sleeves rolled up, a quart of sweat dripping down his neck, and a dark band of it circling his hat.

"I've been fixing a flat," he explains. "Is your mother home?"

"She's in the kitchen, but trust me, she doesn't know the first thing about changing tires."

"Oh, I can handle the tire. I just wonder if she'd bring me a nice, tall glass of water. It's mighty hot out there."

I could go for the water myself, but I'm nervous about leaving this guy in our front hall. What if he's a robber casing our joint? So I yell, "Mom! There's a man out here needs a glass of ice water."

Mom comes out with the glass, and the guy says, "Dr. Rafner? Rosalie Wieitz Rafner?"

How's he know her name? Maybe he was one of her students a long time ago.

"Yes?" Mom offers him the glass.

He reaches into his back pocket and pulls out an envelope with an official seal. "Subpoena from SISS, ma'am," and he slaps the envelope into Mom's hand.

Water flies everywhere.

The guy turns on his heels.

Mom rips the envelope open, and I read it over her shoulder:

One ROSALIE WEITZ, also known as ROSALIE RAFNER, is hereby summoned to be and appear before the Internal Security Sub-Committee of the United States Senate, of which the Honorable William Jenner of Wisconsin is chairman, in a special session to be held in New York on June 3, 1953, at the hour of 9:00 A.M.

There's more, but we both sink into chairs and can't handle it all at once. Mom stashes it in the junk drawer with unidentifiable keys and old trading stamps and other random stuff we never throw away.

The doorbell rings again, and my first impulse is to dash out the back door. But I don't. This time it's just the mailman. Nervously glancing across the street at the feds, he slips me a special delivery envelope addressed to Mom, with no return address, but postmarked from Poughkeepsie, New York. My antenna goes up. Another threat?

"What else can they do to me?" Mom says with a weary sigh. "I have a bad feeling about this."

"Let me open it, Mom, and if it's something disgusting, I'll swallow it." That gets a weary sigh out of her.

Folded inside is a piece of onionskin paper with a short note typed on it: *For your New York expenses. From Friends of McCarran and Smith Act Victims.*

Wrapped in that onionskin is a bank draft for three-hundred dollars. No name, no address.

"I'm not swallowing this!"

"I'm touched," Mom murmurs. "I've heard they take care of people who are forced to testify, but how could they have known since I just got the subpoena?" She catches her breath. "Oh, they've got people planted on the inside." Spies of the spies. She fans herself with the check. "It's also a kind of bribe, isn't it, Marty? Guaranteeing that I don't name names? But I'm going to assume it's a gesture of support, and God knows, we need support."

CHAPTER 23
TUESDAY, MAY 19 –
WEDNESDAY, MAY 20

I have a sudden inspiration to clear my fuzzy brain, so I run over to the College. Been doing that a lot lately, as if I'm missing Hawthorne already in Poland.

The afternoon sun's fried the lawn around Whittier Tower. Even the make-out artists usually rolling around in the grass have the sense to stay in the shade, so no one sees me unlock the tower door. This time I pace myself climbing the winding stairs, and when I finally reach the top, I'm pumped with energy.

Beautiful up here, but terrifying. The platform is pentagon-shaped. I find the exact middle under the bell and spread my legs to root myself here, safe from the wind, with my arms spread wide. They're wings. I could actually fly off this tower. The wind would carry me awhile before I went into freefall and had the fantastic feeling of letting myself go to the forces of nature.

Instead I just do a three-sixty, hands up, feeling the weight of the wind on my palms and sucking in the breeze that never stops blowing here on the Kansas plains.

I'm totally alone, but not lonely. I am free as the wind. If that's not power, I don't know what is.

◊

The next day, Mom is still in her enraged army cook phase, slamming a pan of peanut butter cookies into the oven and hurling fuzzy leftovers from the fridge across the room into the garbage. She doesn't bother giving me a disapproving glare when I scoop fingers of cookie dough into my mouth. Now she's got her face buried in a head of lettuce. Not a good sign.

The back door starts jumping with somebody's fist pounding at it. Mom sucks in a bunch of loose stuff in her throat and dries her eyes with a dish towel. As I open the door, Amy Lynn falls into the kitchen. She's soaked, and her shoes squish on our linoleum.

"It's raining torrents out there! I climbed the fence and ran through your sloshy backyard to sneak over here so *they* wouldn't see me." Finger jabs toward the front of the house, meaning the FBI, and she whispers, "We waited all night to hear from Pop. He's gone. Vanished!"

Before Amy Lynn can say more, Mom clutches her shoulders and pantomimes *We're going out to the backyard so we can talk freely.*

Outside we huddle at the picnic table, with newspapers tented over our heads against the rain.

"Now, tell me what's happened," Mom says.

Between sobs, Amy Lynn sputters and gasps through the story. "Yesterday they sent him to jail! But this morning they let him out to work with his lawyer for the wind-up of the hearing. He promised to call us the minute he was free. We never heard from him and neither did his lawyer."

I pull the dish towel off Rosalie's shoulder and hand it to Amy Lynn to soak up her tears. She gives me a weak smile, smears the cloth across her face, then jams the soggy thing back in my hand.

"And?" Mom says calmly. "Take a deep breath and tell me the rest."

"Okay, all right. So the lawyer's staff called everyone, the police, the FBI, hospitals, all that kind of stuff. He's not *anywhere*! My mother's frantic. She's calling everybody they ever knew. Mother thinks the FBI's got him. I think he's been kidnapped for ransom, or he has amnesia, or, oh, God, he could be lying in a ditch right now, half dead. Nine hours have passed since he left the jail. *Nine hours!*"

"There's got to be a logical explanation." Mom pushes the back door open and yells, "Irwin, could you come out here and kill this *carnivorous* centipede?" Clever, my mom.

He recognizes the code word, comes flying and makes Amy Lynn repeat the whole story. By now we're all drenched. I run inside for a glass of milk for her and pull a smoking pan of cookies out of the oven. Back outside, handing her a stack of blackened cookies, I say dumb stuff like, "Don't worry, he'll turn up. He probably just went bowling or something." Bowling? How'd I come up with that?

Everybody looks grim.

"Irwin, any thoughts you'd care to share?" asks Mom.

"Theo and I touched on something. A radical plan." His eyes flick between Mom and me. "I said something to you about it, remember?"

Yeah, the word *disappear* pops into my mind, in Dad's voice.

Amy Lynn brightens. "You know where he is, Dr. Irwin?"

"No." Dad hunches forward and whispers, "I suspect he's gone underground."

Prairie dogs go underground, moles, potatoes, root cellars, gophers, coffins. Not somebody's living-breathing father.

"What's that mean, Dr. Irwin, *underground*?"

"Some of his compatriots spirited him to safety. They're hiding him. He's in good hands."

"You mean in communist hands, Dr. Irwin?"

He ignores this and says, "I'm sure he's safe, Amy Lynn. Safe from harm, and safe from the clutches of the government. When the time is right, you'll get a message from him. For now, let's go talk to your mother together." He starts out the garden gate with her; he's not going to be catapulting over the back fence. Then he looks over his shoulder. "Martin, why don't you stop by the Sonfelters' house a little later today? Amy Lynn could use a friend."

◊

Man, so could Mom. All the lawyers are fussing over Mom and arguing with one another in the attic war room. They're spooked by Dr. Sonfelter's disappearance. And now that Mom's actually been summoned, the stakes are higher. More legal beagles are swarming in and out of the house.

"At least we're not paying *them*," Dad says, as a bunch of law students thunder up the stairs to the attic.

I wish I knew where the *friends* hide fugitives who go AWOL, in case we need to find Mom if she vanishes into thin air.

Seems like now would be a good time to check in with Amy Lynn. I take her Mom's latest kitchen disaster, a beef steak and kidney pie that weighs as much as a tire. Amy Lynn and I toss around some stupid talk, until, trying to sound real casual, I say, "Oh, by the way, been meaning to tell you, my mom got her summons to testify."

"No!" Amy Lynn shrieks. "I can't go through this again."

Burns me a little, because *she's* not going through it; I am. "So, we're going to New York in a couple weeks for the hearing. Different committee, but just as rank. Oh, yeah, and they might deport her. Next month we could be living in Poland."

"*Poland*?" Amy Lynn drops the pie; I catch it on the first bounce. It's indestructible.

CHAPTER 24
FRIDAY, MAY 22

The Yankees/White Sox game in Chicago: that's what I've got to zero in on, instead of Mom's hearing and the scheming and strategizing and yelling that pour out of our attic.

It's not working. I break out the memos.

From the desk of
IRWIN RAFNER, Ph.D.'s son Marty

DATE: May 22, 1953

TO: Mickey Mantle

Guess what, Mick? I'm gonna see you play next week. White Sox at Yankee Stadium, June 2. Except it's only because the feds are building a case against my mom. I've been thinking about this a lot. What if the SISS guy comes down hard and she's sentenced to—

I scratch out that last bit. I can't put the words out there in the sunlight. For the first time I get it, I understand why Luke can't say the things that eat him up inside.

We could all end up in Poland, Mick. They don't even play Triple A minor league in Poland.

◊

I've been keeping a close watch on the Everlys since I heard Wendy was planning to split. Man, the FBI could hire me as a part-time spy. I need a summer job.

Luke and Wendy are having a fight. At least it gets him talking. She's flinging her hands in the air, jabbing her finger into Luke's chest, and dragging Carrie around, glopped on to her leg. Next thing, Wendy stashes Carrie into the car and screeches up Oxbow Road.

Luke will just sit there as usual, sure. But after a minute he leaps out of his chair, lets out an agonizing wolf howl, jumps a couple feet in the air, and grabs the basketball ring hanging over the garage. He's swinging from it until it rips away from the wall. He comes whooping down with his arms wrapped around the orange ring, hollering at the top of his lungs. Drops to the ground. Whoa! He's rolling down the driveway!

I sprint across the street and grab him before he hits the muddy gutter. "You okay, Luke?" Stupid question. Gimme something better to say.

He turns his eyes up to me, the eyes I expect to be not there, as usual, but they're screwed into small, dark bullets of rage, which he fires my way.

"Hey, sorry, man!" I back off.

Milgrim's out of the car now. "Need help, kid?"

"Not from you."

Luke hurls that basketball ring as hard as he can. It makes a sharp dent in the driver's door of the Studebaker.

"Hey!" Kluski jumps out.

My heart stampedes as I pick up the hoop and clutch it to my chest. If they want to confiscate it for proof of an attack on government property, they'll have to claw through last night's corn chowder to pull it out of our trash can.

Luke stomps up and down the driveway, yowling like a tomcat. His chest heaves so hard that you can see his heart thumping through his T-shirt. What if he has a heart attack? My mind races through that first-aid movie we saw in gym, *Disaster on a Hunting Trip*. How to do artificial respiration. Mouth-to-mouth. Pinch the nostrils while you breathe in? How many breaths? Pound the chest? Turn on his side—left or right?

It's a blurry splash of images: snake bite, tourniquets, drowning, bleeding, shock. Panic rises in my own chest.

Milgrim comes closer, Kluski right behind him. Milgrim locks his hands around Luke's shoulders. "Easy does it, sir. Calm down, breathe shallow . . . " He lowers Luke to the lawn chair. "Head down between your knees, sir. There, good. Pulse slowing, slowing. Steady. There you go, Corporal Everly. You're out of the woods."

The two feds back down the driveway. I don't move until I hear the car door slam. Down on my knees, I look into Luke's hard eyes. "You doing better now?"

He raises his head, nods slowly, and says, "They're . . . leaving . . . me."

A wave of pure grief shudders through me. "I heard, Luke. Let's go inside."

He falls asleep on the couch in the front room. I listen to him breathe until shadows darken the room, then head home.

CHAPTER 25
FRIDAY, MAY 22

The legal pit crew's gone for the day, leaving a colossal mess of scummy cups, food wrappers and balled-up paper and paper airplanes all over the attic. Bubbie Sylvia just called; she's still tearing through her boxes; no citizenship papers yet. She called the Chicago immigration office, where she remembers taking the oath of citizenship, but they have no record of it. Did she just imagine it? Was it a lie all along? Or did the FBI pull the records?

Dad drags me into the john for the latest heated family discussion, already in progress. *We return you now to your regularly scheduled program.*

He and I sit at the edge of the bathtub, while Mom perches on the toilet lid. Just your average American family terrorized by the FBI.

I'm still shook up about Luke, but they're caught up in their own stuff. It's sweltering in here, and we don't dare open the window. Bath water sloshing and banking off the tub hits my face with a refreshing mist almost as good as running through a sprinkler. We talk in whispers and hand signals and lip-reading.

Dad buries his face in a towel that muffles his words. "Quincy thinks your mother should consider ducking the SISS hearing, and we take off for Mexico. Lots of expatriates south of the border."

"No!" I'll bet nobody in Tijuana or Juarez plays baseball worth spit. Not thinking straight. There's more at stake here than pop flies and peanuts and Cracker Jacks.

"Mexico won't work for us," Mom says, to my relief. "It would be hard to make a decent wage teaching, and we could never come back across the border."

"There's that other option." I glance at the window casually, like it's not something that's been keeping me up at night and raising hives on my belly. "You could go underground, like Amy Lynn's father did." Somewhere nearby—not Mexico. Western Kansas? They'd never find us out there.

"Sure, and what about the rest of you? I'd be miserable without you, and you'd miss my home cooking."

I can't believe she's still cracking jokes, still stubborn as a mule, at a time like this.

Mom reaches over and pats my knee, which makes me feel babyish. "It's a viable option. Better than deportation. But I still think I should face the committee."

Suddenly my chaotic family, the attic lawyers, Amy Lynn and her vanishing-act father, Wendy and Carrie, and Luke yowling and rolling down the driveway—the white-hot rage of it hits me so hard that I'm staggering and gasping for breath.

"Calm down, Martin," Dad says in that got-it-together voice I hate.

"No! I won't calm down! Have you thought about me? Either of you? Given a single thought to what's good for ME? That's what parents are supposed to do, in case you haven't heard."

Mom's face is blurred by my tears, but I can still see that I've hurt her more than the Carnivore or the FBI or the SISS guys or anybody could. She doesn't say a word, just looks at me with her eyes swimming, her palm cupped to her lips. I should shut up. I can't.

"Why don't you just go ahead and take off for Guadalajara—or Warsaw, for all I care. Just leave me here to fend for myself!"

Dad's eyes are flaring; he frantically taps his lips with his index finger, but I don't care if those creeps across the street in their pee-fermented car hear every rotten word I'm shouting.

"Totally selfish, that's what you are! It's all about your *principles*, your *conscience*, your *options*. You keep talking about options and *viable plans*. Well, I got news for you. All of 'em stink!"

I . . . can't catch my breath . . . choking . . . gonna topple like a dead cottonwood . . . fall into the bath-tub . . . drown . . . you can drown in two inches of water . . . mouth-to-mouth . . .

Dad grabs me, but I tear away from him and holler, "THEY COULD EXECUTE YOU, MOM, LIKE THEY'RE DOING TO THE ROSENBERGS!"

◊

When I open my eyes, I'm lying on the bathroom floor with an ice pack across my forehead. Mom rubs my arms. Furry-headed and dizzy, my first thought is, *She's not in Sing Sing with the Rosenbergs. Not on Death Row.*

The water's splashing. We're all soaked. Dad squats beside me. His shimmering face comes into focus like a reflection in a river. His voice echoes down a long tunnel: "Martin? Can you hear me?"

Words form in my throat, but can't pass my tongue, same as Luke. Two pairs of eyes loom over me.

"Marty?" Mom's voice. "You're scaring me. Say something."

"Something," I mutter, trying to sit up. "Sorry about—"

Mom strokes my face. "It's okay, Marty. It had to be said. You're right, there are no good choices. But we'll work it all out, I promise."

"How can you promise, Mom?"

"Shh, just take it easy for now."

Like Luke, like Luke and Milgrim.

They prop me up against the wall, one on each side. Now that those terrifying words—*They could execute you,*

Mom—have finally broken free of my head I'm feeling some relief. The water's still crashing against the tub walls and my head's still spinning, but I'm starting to breathe like a regular person again. Like Luke.

"Okay," I say finally, "why not do the SISS thing? The lawyers have been prepping you round the clock. You're ready for anything they sling your way." I hope.

If not, she can pull a Theo Sonfelter and disappear.

We're in a miserable bind no matter which way you slice it, but I'd rather put Dr. Rosalie in the game than bench her before it even starts.

CHAPTER 26
FRIDAY, MAY 29 –
SUNDAY, MAY 31

'*'ve had a week to recover from my freak-out, and now the day is here. Watching my eyes spin in the mirror, I'm thinking, why isn't there a law against having to catch a train at four in the morning?

Mom, Dad, me, Quincy, and Vic all jam our sleepy bodies and our luggage into the DeSoto. The guys in the Studebaker are elbowing each other awake. They'll probably follow us to Newton, where we'll catch the train—or even all the way to New York. *Take a couple days' vacation,* I want to holler, *'cause there's not much action on Oxbow Road while the menacing Rafners are on the loose.*

Every mile the sky gets brighter with a spectacular sunrise light show. We're heading east into the sun, but I can't look away as we chug-a-chug across the plains. I guess the Rosenbergs don't get to fry their eyeballs; no sun in Sing Sing Prison.

I hang out in the lounge car with Vic, watching lots of real estate streak by. It's mostly wheat fields and tractor yards so far, and a few cows grazing and lapping at streams. What a boring life.

No chance Vic will get interesting soon, so I keep thinking that every mile puts us that much closer to the Yankees game Mom promised me.

By mid-morning we'll hit Chicago, home of the White Sox, and then collect more train cars and a thousand miles, straight into Penn Station, New York City, USA. Yankees territory. Good thing about the Yanks: they don't care who's a pinko commie, as long as he hits homers or pitches lightning curves and fastballs.

Last night I oiled my glove and tied it around a nice seasoned baseball so it'll be ripe and ready for my first major league game, just in case Mantle hits a homer to me, or even a foul. A minute ago I showed the mitt to Vic. His idea of sports is two guys hunched over podiums arguing about which is worse, DDT sprayed on the lettuce crop that migrant workers pick, or wormy lettuce without DDT. We're on our thousandth game of gin in the lounge car. At every stop more passengers board, most of them Rosenberg People heading for New York to join demonstrations against the execution. Twenty days left.

Once the Rosenberg People hear that Mom is on her way to testify, presto, she's a celeb, and they're firing advice at her.

A couple of nuns hover close. One says, "Be stalwart and steadfast."

The other grabs Mom's hands and pumps them like

she's drawing water. "God will give you the strength to get through this ordeal. Remember the courage of Julius and Ethel as they walk through the valley of the shadow of death."

Other Rosenberg People aren't so gentle.: "Don't give them *any* names," one fiercely bearded man warns. "Swear on this bible." He pulls Mom's right hand on to a book so small that it's got to be the *Readers Digest* condensed version.

How do you like this? It turns out to be a bound copy of the Constitution, which Mom's always quoting like she wrote it herself.

She pulls her hand back and looks that man in the eye. "If I got into this morass by refusing to sign a loyalty oath, I must also refuse to swear on your bible, as much as I uphold its truths, my friend."

Vic slaps cards down on the table. "That mother of yours is one stubborn lady."

After dinner, which is all stiff white tablecloths and silvery plates, Mom and Dad turn in to get her cranked up for the hearing, or calmed down, or whatever it takes.

A girl named Janine lures us into a songfest with a new kind of candy bar called Rocky Road. One bite of that soft chocolate-covered marshmallow, and I'm hooked. I could eat thirty of 'em and probably puke all the way to New York.

Janine asks, "You know any union songs?"

"Nope."

"Any Weavers? Guthrie? Any Paul Robeson?"

"Uh-uh." Communists all, that's what the newspapers say, and Milgrim and Dimple Chin would be the first to second that motion.

"That's all right. You'll catch on!" In a minute we're singing in rounds, *Wim-o-weh, o-wim-o-weh , wim-o-weh, o-wim-o-weh . . . in the jungle, the mighty jungle, the lion sleeps tonight . . .*

It doesn't seem like a commie song, and neither does "If I Had a Hammer." I snarf another Rocky Road.

Who'd guess it? Vic turns out to be a ham. He's loosened his tie and he's standing on a table warbling *"Good night Irene, good night Irene, I'll see you in my dreams . . ."*

After all that wild singing, someone flips a switch. Suddenly it's all about the Rosenbergs.

"Framed, clear and simple!" a pony-tailed woman from Seattle yells, "and nobody cares."

"Nobody?" some guy shoots back. "There are ten thousand people in D.C. right now demonstrating against this gross miscarriage of justice. There are Rosenberg Committees in every city in America and half the countries of the world! Whaddaya mean *nobody*?"

"That low-down stoolpigeon, David Greenglass, how could he send his sister to the chair to save his own neck?"

". . . the fact that the Rosenbergs were sentenced to death by one judge and no jury, why, it's unconscionable."

". . . and a Jewish judge, at that," says a man with a black yarmulke on his head.

Judge Kaufman is Jewish? Like Mr. and Mrs. Rosenberg? Like us? How could he do it to one of his own? Oh, yeah, as Dad once said, "Justice is blind," to which Mom added, "Deaf and dumb, too, in this case."

They're all shouting and crying and pounding each other on the back, when a man who'd been sitting quietly in the corner suddenly tosses his newspaper across the room and launches into his tirade: "I've heard enough of this commie-kissing claptrap. Youse each one oughta be deported to the Soviet Union and kicked by the seat of your pants into one of them Russian labor camps to rot your pinko hide for the next fifty years. Matter of fact, you can all just march alongside your traitorous Jew-martyrs, and I hope, come June 18, they're fried as crisp as cheap bacon."

I knock over a chair leaping to my feet. I'm gonna punch the guy's lights out! Me, who's never even been in a schoolyard fight.

Vic clenches my arm, shaking his head frantically. Any other group would pounce on the creep and beat him bloody. Not the Rosenberg People. They're all about nonviolence and justice and free speech. So they let him rant his hatred and stomp out of the lounge car on his own two feet, leaving us in stunned silence.

The Seattle woman picks up his newspaper and rips it to shreds. That's as violent as this crowd gets.

Later, tucked between the tight, starched-stiff sheets of my bunk, I try to lose that man's vicious words behind a mess of baseball stats, which, for the first time in my life, doesn't work. The clatter of the train rattling along the tracks reminds me that we're getting closer to New York and Mom's hearing.

And the scary truth is, Mr. and Mrs. Rosenberg are rounding third and heading toward home, only they're going to be tagged out. Game over.

The old question resurfaces. What if they frame Mom just like the Rosenbergs, and she goes to trial and they pin a bunch of lies on her, and she gets sentenced to death by electrocution? Fear grabs me and shakes me like a tree in a tornado.

But suddenly, rattling down the track, an odd change comes over me, as if I've turned a corner into a space cadet's parallel universe. Just like this train's coal turns to steam, that fear that's been gripping me is converted to . . . I don't know what to call this, how I'm feeling. It has to do with Mom's conscience about what's right and what's wrong, and Dad's determination to stand by her even though he's mad that her loyalty oath thing got us into this big, fat black hole.

The thing is, I'm them; they're me, their only kid. For sure, I can be spitting mad at them, but I'm also proud of the way they stick to their principles and stick by each other.

Pride, yeah, that's what I'm feeling. We're Team Rafner.

CHAPTER 27
TUESDAY, JUNE 2 – WEDNESDAY, JUNE 3

June. Before this month's out, the Rosenbergs will be dead. But I gotta shove that aside, because here I am in da Bronx, following the swarm into the ball park. Never saw so many people in one place. I swear, everybody who's not in London packing the stands for the coronation of Queen Elizabeth is right here, in Yankee Stadium. Feels like one of those fuzzy dream scenes in the movies, where some actor twirls dizzily and walks on air instead of solid, gritty ground.

I'm sure the Mick can smell that Marty Rafner's in the ballpark, even though we're in cheap seats about two miles up from leftfield. But hey, you get a bird's eye view of the whole field.

It's okay if he's off his game. He doesn't have to hit a homer for me. But when Mickey strikes out his first at-bat, my heart sinks to the beer-puddled ground already paved with peanut shells.

The game's lost on my parents. Every so often Mom lifts her head out of the book she's reading and asks a ridiculous question, such as "How can you tell who's who when they're all wearing caps?"

Dad's brow is wrinkled as he watches every pitch, every play so seriously and tries to clap and cheer at the right times, but he's always a beat off. He even slugs back a beer like one of the guys and forgets to wipe the foam off his lip. He ends up studying the program as if Casey Stengel is gonna give him a pop quiz before they'll let us out of the ballpark.

I'm pinching myself to be sure it's not all a dream. Joe Dobson's pitching for the White Sox, and he's not half bad, I gotta admit, until he hurls one that the Mick cracks loud and solid into left field and squeezes out a double. Incredible!

For a few hours, I forget about the Rosenbergs and about Mom facing snipers at the hearing tomorrow. For this one hot, sticky, sunburnt, Yankee Stadium after-noon, everything is peachy perfect. It's neck-and-neck all nine innings, until the Yankees pull a win out on a steal by Yogi Berra in the bottom of the tenth, and the Sox don't have another chance to bite the Yankees' rears. Sweet victory!

In my knapsack are two baseball cards: a Mantle rookie and a 1949 Rizzuto. What are my chances of get-ting one of the cards autographed? Fans pour onto the field before I can leap down from the nosebleed stands. The Mick is swarmed, six circles deep, but maybe I can get to Phil Rizzuto, who's open, compared to Mantle.

I slip the mint-condition card out of the cellophane protector and wave it over the heads of a lot of other kids. "Mr. Rizzuto? Hey, Scooter, over here!"

He glances up from signing a ball and makes eye contact. I push my way toward him, elbowing every other baseball fanatic out of the way. "Sir, can you sign this for my friend? He's a Korean War vet, and you're tops with him." I hand Rizzuto the card and a piece of paper with Luke's name on it.

The man has class. He's a lot older than Mantle, but he flashes a boyish grin and signs:

For Luke Everly,
Your country's proud of you.
Phil (Scooter) Rizzuto 6/2/53

You gotta love the guy. I'm plenty satisfied, though I never even get close enough to Mickey Mantle to smell the sweat dripping off his chin.

◊

The three of us are staying in one hotel room to save money. The three-hundred-dollar windfall from the *friends* is nearly gone on train tickets and meals and this hotel. Believe me, this isn't the Ritz, but at least the toilet flushes and we each get a bite-sized bar of Ivory soap, free.

I bunk on the lumpy hide-a-bed couch. We're all pretty restless, and once I woke up and found Mom not exactly sleepwalking, but pacing the room, which, as Bubbie Sylvia would say, is so small that you have to go outside to change your mind.

Somehow we get through the night.

Nobody wants breakfast; too nervous. Competition for the bathroom is deadly. Dad's first, then me, and finally we turn the plumbing and mirror over to Mom. A long time passes, and tension's thick enough to chip off in chunks like Fleet bubble gum.

Dad and I sit next to each other on the folded-up couch like the wise monkeys, See-No-Evil and Hear-No-Evil, but we're missing Speak-No-Evil. She's still in the bathroom.

My favorite nervous habit: I work a little hole in the upholstery and dig for stuffing like it's gold. My hair is slicked back, and that stupid commercial jingle keeps racing through my mind: *Brylcreem, a little dab'll do ya. Use more, only if you dare.* I've gooped on more than a dab, and my hair won't move if a cyclone rips through the room.

We jump about a yard when the phone *brrrrring*s. It's Bubbie, still scrounging through the boxes in her basement, looking for the citizenship papers.

"Anything?" Dad asks hopefully, and then his face sags. "We have to be at the hearing in thirty minutes. We'll call you later, Sylvia. Afterward," he promises.

There's nothing else to say, so we sit quietly in the two-man monkey row.

Steam pours out when Mom opens the bathroom door, and when the steam clears, I can't believe what I see: a real nice-looking lady in a skinny sky-blue suit and pointy high heels. La-di-da clothes like she said she wouldn't want to be buried in.

Surprise! She has legs, she has a waistline. Who'd have guessed? She also has fake rosy cheeks and lips coated with glossy red stuff, and her brownish-gray hair that usually hangs down her back in a braid is now swept up into a complicated bird's nest.

She twirls around like a model. "What do you think?"

"Sheesh, Mom, you look like a female!"

She bites open a bobby pin and plants it up under the nest on her head. Maybe she's afraid her hair will try to escape. I wouldn't blame it; it looks like it hurts, cruelly twisted up that way, like if you're arm-wrestling and bend too far the wrong way.

Dad swallows a couple of times. "You look gorgeous, Rosie, just stunning." Man, I haven't heard him call her Rosie in months. He sweeps her into his arms, waltzing her around the room, tripping over my feet and the floor lamp jutting out of a corner.

It's time. Gulp. Mom picks up her small train case.

I stare at the case as if its locks might snap open and a saltwater-spitting iguana would come shooting out. "Is that what I think it's for?"

She nods. "Toothbrush, change of underwear, my poetry manuscript, lots of pens and ink. Just in case."

Just in case they take her right to jail from the SISS hearing.

CHAPTER 28
WEDNESDAY, JUNE 3

The hearing is in a huge downtown hotel. Giant glass chandeliers hang from the ceiling. If one falls, it'll be instant death. That'll save us a lot of trouble.

"Knock 'em dead, Mom." I straighten the scarf around her neck, Dad kisses her cheek, and we send her off into battle with the U.S. Senate.

It's not easy for her to walk in those spiked heels. Still, when Mr. Quincy takes her arm, she marches right into that hearing room like a pitcher to his mound. The room is already crowded. A small herd of reporters sits up close, and a couple of photographers stand on tables to snap pictures from every weird angle. We're stuck in a back row where Vic has reserved seats for us.

Mom's on her own now. The first hurdle is when they ask her to swear on a Bible.

". . . The truth, the whole truth, and nothing but the truth, so help you God?"

She hesitates with her hand hovering over the book. Dad groans. We stop breathing in the echoey silence of the room until Mom lays her hand on the book and says, "I do." It costs her a bundle of self-respect to take the senators' oath, but she isn't ready to rock the boat yet. She's saving her best stuff for later.

I try to listen to everything, but those senators are spouting words the way whales spout water through their blowholes. So I tune in and out, like when you're doing homework and listening to a game on the radio, and the ump's calling nothing but balls.

Here's some of what I catch, with Mom answering yes sir, no sir, and when she tries to say more, they cut her off.

"You stated your name as Rosalie Rafner, correct? Mrs. Rafner, have you ever used an alias? No? Then would you explain who Rosalie Weitz is? Weitz is a Polish name, is it not?"

We know where the guy's going with this Polish stuff.

"I earned my doctorate under my maiden name, Weitz, before I was married, Senator."

"Isn't it true that you're known around Hawthorne College as Professor Rafner, and not Professor Weitz?"

"That is only for consistency, sir, as my husband and son carry the Rafner name."

"Ah, so you *do* use an alias."

You can see the senators keeping mental scorecards. That's the way it goes, with them trying to catch her on their hooks. When they hit on the loyalty oath thing,

Dad squeezes my hand until it feels like the fingers are gonna snap off and thud to the floor.

"Mrs. Rafner, could you please state for the committee why you've stubbornly refused to sign a simple loyalty oath at the college that employs you?"

She's memorized a speech for this question. "Gentlemen, it is my contention that university loyalty oaths are objectionable on three separate grounds. First, they are contrary to academic freedom, restricting what one may think and teach. Second—"

One of the senators butts in: "You teach at a Quaker college, correct? Quakers are known to oppose oaths, yet we don't hear you objecting on religious grounds."

"I am not a Quaker, sir."

"What religion *are* you, Mrs. Rafner?"

"With all due respect, sir, I believe that information is irrelevant. However, in the interest of cooperation, I'll tell you that I am Jewish. Regardless, I support the Quaker belief that the integrity of a person's word is good enough without swearing an oath."

"Yet you swore on the Bible," one senator says with a smirk.

"I did, yes. Otherwise we couldn't have even begun these proceedings. My second objection—"

"I believe you've made your objections quite clear already," another senator says, puffing away on a cigar.

"Sir, I have a point to make, if you please." Before he can protest, Mom plows on. "My second contention is that loyalty oaths are contrary to the United States Constitution, which, as you well know, guarantees the liberties of freedom of speech, freedom of assembly, and the freedom to redress justifiable grievances against the government."

"Why'd she say that?" Vic whimpers.

The chairman jumps on that statement. "May I assume, then, that you have grievances against the government of this country?"

"No, sir, no more than any other patriotic citizen."

The pot boils. Mom calling herself patriotic must have ticked them off. "Are you now, or have you ever been, a member of a communist organization, or any organization dedicated to the violent overthrow of the United States government?"

"Violent overthrow, never. Your thinking may differ from mine as to what defines a communist—"

"Are you a member of a labor union?"

"A college teachers' union, yes, but I hardly think—"

"Are you familiar with the Institute for Pacific Relations, known as the IPR?"

"Vaguely."

"And are you aware that the IPR perpetrated the fall of China to the communists in 1949?"

"No, sir, that is not within my range of knowledge."

"Mrs. Rafner, exactly what *is* within your range of knowledge regarding the IPR? More simply, what is your affiliation with that nefarious organization?"

"Minimal. I merely translated a Chinese poem for one of the members."

"Ah! You speak Chinese!"

"No native speaker would recognize it as such. What I have is a modest reading knowledge from my college minor in Asian literature. Just enough to translate a simple poem."

"Are you aware that the IPR has been under investigation for more than a year, thus bringing your link with the organization into question?"

"Respectfully, sir, the poem I translated was the lament of a fourteenth-century lovesick maiden. Hardly subversive material, Senator."

He turns a sharp corner. "We'll make it simple for you, Mrs. Rafner. Are you now a member of a communist organization or a communist front organization? I remind you, you are under oath."

Quincy and Mom huddle. I suck in my breath, like I'm underwater with her, swimming in a barracuda-infested sea. If she says yes, she'll be drawn into the undertow, but before she sinks, they'll pump her for names of other people. If she says no, and they connect her with some group they *claim* is communist, she'll be lunch for the barracudas, because they can nail her for perjury, which is lying under oath. Jail time. Even though she *isn't* lying. No wonder people don't want to take oaths.

Mr. Quincy pushes his chair back and stands tall. "Senators, before my client answers further questions, she wants the record to show that she wishes to stand by a diminished Fifth Amendment."

"Diminished, sir?"

"Yes, Senator. By that we mean, to the best of Mrs. Rafner's knowledge and recollection, she will truthfully answer questions pertaining to herself, but will not answer questions pertaining to other people."

The senator is practically barking now. "May I remind you that there is no such thing as a diminished Fifth."

"Nevertheless," Mr. Quincy says with a defeated sigh.

Uh-oh, riptide time. It's sink or swim now.

CHAPTER 29
WEDNESDAY, JUNE 3

The chairman's comments are getting more and more snide. "Allow me to rephrase the previous question for elegance, Mrs. Rafner. Are you currently a member of the Communist Party USA?"

"Mr. Chairman, please let the record show that I ardently object to that question—"

"Are you, or are you not?" He's just about spitting into the mic now.

"If you would let me finish my sentence, Senator, you would have your response."

"Which is what?"

"I am not."

"Not what?"

"I am not a member of the Communist Party USA."

Phew! She's finally said it!

Vic whispers, "Note the wording. She's being very precise and specific."

The chairman's no numbskull. "Are you a member of any *other* communist party, domestic or international."

"I am not.'"

Okay, home free—but one look at Dad tells me the inning could end with Mom stuck on base.

Now the senator's breathing the words into the mic. "Have you *ever* been a member of a communist organization, domestic or international?"

Mom hesitates so she can choose the right words, like a true poet.

"Are you hedging? Are you refusing to answer the question?"

"No, sir, I am neither hedging nor refusing, although I repeat, I object to this line of questioning as a constitutional violation. Nevertheless, my answer: The FBI has informed me that two groups with which I was briefly affiliated, perhaps ten years ago, are on the dubious list of communist front organizations, although I do not believe they merit that designation, nor was I engaged in any communist activity while—"

The chairman flips through a stack of pages. "Might the groups you're referring to be the Congress of American Women and the National Council of the Arts, Sciences, and Professions?"

"Yes, Mr. Chairman. Both groups have no political motivations other than to promote professional standards and equity for—"

Well, next they start asking if she knows a billion other people who've been members, and who they say also belong to commie organizations.

After each name Mom says, "I respectfully decline to respond, according to my Fifth Amendment rights."

Name after name, *respectfully decline*, until the chairman growls, "Let the record show that Mrs. Rafner is a most unfriendly witness. Diminished Fifth, indeed."

Like Yogi Berra says, baseball is ninety per cent mental, the other half physical. Mom's holding her own mentally. Barely touching First with her big toe, she's ready to steal.

Me, I'm not doing so well. With my feet propped on Mom's train case, and the overhead fans whirling, and the flashbulbs firing, and Dad clutching my arm, I am sweating like a warthog. Is this how Robby and Michael Rosenberg felt when their parents were on the stand?

Scared or not, my stomach's growling. Sheesh, did the senators hear it? Because the chairman says, "Mrs. Rafner, we shall adjourn for lunch and reconvene in this room in ninety minutes. Promptly." The gavel banging echoes through the room, and Mom stands up, wobbly on those pointy heels.

"Mrs. Rafner! Dr. Weitz! Rosalie!" Reporters in the hall stick microphones in her face and call her by every name except Lassie to get her attention, but Quincy and Vic make sure nobody says a word as we're herded out to Broadway.

One Associated Press guy stops us in our tracks, though. "Did you hear the news from Sing Sing? The

Supreme Court ruled against the Rosenbergs' latest appeal for a stay of execution. Comment?"

Mom tries not to react, but she mutters under her breath, "Now their only hope is an appeal to Eisenhower for clemency. Good God."

All the newsies scribble down that comment, of course.

Things are looking grim for the home team. We hoof it back to the hotel coffee shop, first stopping for messages. Bubbie Sylvia called twice.

"You'd better call back, Rosie. Maybe she has something."

Mom steps into the phone booth in the lobby. The rest of us, including the lawyers, cluster around the booth. A fistful of change jingles down the throat of the pay phone. It's hard to read her face, and her hands are waving around like they always do when she talks to Bubbie—somewhere between a hug and a slug.

She lets the phone dangle by the cord and pushes her way out of the booth. I rush in after her.

"Bubbie?" I yell into the phone. "What's going on?"

"Oy, sweetheart, I've been through every inch of the storage locker, every carton, every drawer, every closet. I even went to my safe deposit box at First Federal. Nothing."

"How's that possible? You remember the day, the certificate, the snapshot."

"Could I have thrown it out? By accident, of course.

I don't know what to do for my Rosalie. Tell me, what's happening there, in the hearing?"

"Mom's holding her own, but they're starting to turn the screws."

"Okay, sweetheart. Listen, I'll just keep looking. Maybe there's some spot I missed. So, you should go have lunch. A nice pickled tongue sandwich, maybe?"

Not a chance. At the hotel coffee shop, lunch is grease with a hamburger patty coagulating in it, inside a soggy bun, and fries that must have been cooked last week.

And now, the seventh inning stretch is over, and we're back in the game. The chairman's warmed up, pitching spitballs and sliders, and we're about to find out if Mom can keep on slugging.

CHAPTER 30
WEDNESDAY, JUNE 3

"Mrs. Rafner, in the matter of one Yossele Mendelev," the chairman begins, "what is your recollection of his residency at Hawthorne College in Kansas?" He wrinkles up his nose as if Kansas smells like the armpit of the universe.

"Dr. Mendelev spent a month at the College teaching master poetry classes," Mom says into the mic.

"In what language did he teach these classes?"

"Not in Russian, if that's what you're getting at, Mr. Chairman. Dr. Mendelev's English is quite intelligible."

One of the other senators leans into his microphone, and his first few words bounce off the walls till he reins in his voice. "I see in our briefing that this Mendelev was a guest in your home for five full weeks, correct?

"Yes, sir, we often provide home hospitality for visiting professors." Hidden message: *even the ones who aren't from Russia*.

"And is it true, Mrs. Rafner, that this professor entertained American students in your home?"

"American as well as international students. Hawthorne is a liberal arts college that attracts students from abroad because of our superb academic environment and generous endowment program."

Eyebrows go up at the mention of three no-no words: *international* and *liberal*, plus *endowment*, which sounds like free education, a commie idea. Dad shifts restlessly next to me.

Another senator gets his licks in. "Are you aware, Mrs. Rafner, that Mr. Mendelev was a double agent, spying for both the Soviet Union and the United States?"

Tactical error: Mom bursts out laughing.

"You're amused?"

"Forgive me, sir, it's just that Dr. Mendelev is one of the least political people I've known. He's oblivious to borders, believing that poetry transcends national walls between people."

"She's biting her own foot," Dad whispers. "That's a profoundly communistic idea, in their estimation."

Yeah, and now two of the senators sit back with self-satisfied grins, until the chairman says, "I notice that you use the present tense, Mrs. Rafner. Are you unaware that Mr. Mendelev met a firing squad, to his extreme disadvantage? Such is life and death in the Soviet Union, madam."

While Mom's still reeling from this news, the committee pitches more questions at her. Did Mendelev talk about his life in Moscow? Did he try to convince

Hawthorne students to visit the USSR? Did he have mysterious absences? Did he *insinuate* Russian foods into our household diet? On and on, with Quincy nodding his okay after every stupid question, until Mom is exhausted and blurts out, "Please allow me to summarize—"

"We are not interested in one of your statements!" the chairman yells.

She jabbers fast, to get a few words in before they muzzle her. "Dr. Yossele Mendelev was a perfect gentleman, respectful of our home and college and students, a brilliant poet, a man of generous spirit—"

"Nor are we interested in his glorious dossier, or a testimonial on his virtues. We are only interested in his suspicious activities as a spy against the United States and his connection to you, a Polish national."

Mom sinks back in her chair. One senator covers his mic and leans toward the chairman for a pitcher/catcher conference.

"One of our distinguished committeemen has a pressing engagement with the ambassador from New Zealand, so we shall have to tidy up this session and invite you to return at nine o'clock tomorrow morning."

Quincy stands up. "Respectfully, gentlemen, I advise you that the Rafner family has a train reservation at three tomorrow afternoon."

The chairman barks, "Sit down, Mr. Quincy. The business of this committee takes precedence over all other obligations. However, in the interest of good sportsmanship, I feel certain that we will conclude this hearing, one way or another, before lunch tomorrow."

The gavel pounds again, sending pencil stubs flying over the committee's desk. This guy knows as much about sportsmanship as Coach Earlywine does. When it's all over, are we gonna file through, slap hands, and say *good game, good game, guys*?

"So, what should we do with the rest of the day?" Mom asks once we're away from the reporters.

It's four o'clock, too late for a museum or checking out the Polo Grounds, where the Giants play, just to see how the other half of New York baseball lives. (I'm a Yankees man; I don't count the Brooklyn Dodgers.)

Dad says, "I'm tired, and you must be exhausted, Rosalie. Let's go back to the room and take a nap before dinner."

A message is waiting for us at the hotel. Mom hands me the note as she kicks off her heels and flops on the bed. "I've been putting my foot in my mouth all day. You call her, Marty."

Bubbie answers and starts right in. "I don't know if it means anything, but I found this little red cardboard envelope with a key in it."

"Key to what, Bubbie?"

"Who knows, sweetheart? It says *YMHA at 92nd and Lexington*. Zeyde and I used to live there in New York."

"YMHA? What's that?"

From the couch, where Dad's sprawled, comes, "Young Men's Hebrew Association. Like a YMCA, but Jewish."

Bubbie says, "You want to go up there and see if it's anything? Maybe years ago my Avrum hid some important stuff in a gym locker. Maybe a million bucks, or, who knows, could be the citizenship papers. That's all I got for you."

"We're out the door!" I shout into the phone, slamming down the receiver.

Dad pulls out his subway map, shows me which train we'll take, which stop.

Outside there must be five thousand people smashed together in Union Square, with more coming and pushing forward. On a milk crate at the center, a man with a giant megaphone stands under an American flag, bellowing to the crowd: "PRESIDENT EISENHOWER, HEAR OUR PLEA. WE DEMAND JUSTICE FOR JULIUS AND ETHEL!"

"JUSTICE, JUSTICE SHALL YOU PURSUE!" the crowd responds as one throbbing voice.

My heart starts to race, beating to the rhythm of a new chant: "CLEMENCY NOW! CLEMENCY NOW!"

Hand-lettered signs on long wooden slats wave above the heads of the frenzied crowd: *CLEMENCY FOR THE ROSENBERGS! DO IT FOR ROBBY AND MICHAEL! FIFTEEN DAYS! IT'S A TRAVESTY! WHERE'S DEMOCRACY?!* A few signs even say

SHAME ON JUDGE KAUFMAN, the judge who sent them to the Chair.

Police with billy clubs rim the crowd, hot to pounce if things spin out of control. A few mad people are dragged away, kicking and screaming, "FREE SPEECH IS DEAD IN AMERICA!"

Dad pushes me through the crowd, quiet beside me, but I'm caught up in the energy, every nerve of my body tingling with excitement, like I really *am* a Rosenberg Person. I'm chanting along with the rest of them: "JUSTICE FOR ETHEL! JUSTICE FOR JULIUS! JUSTICE FOR ETHEL! JUSTICE FOR JULIUS!"

"Marty?" Dad taps my shoulder to snap me out of it. "We have to get uptown to the YMHA before the office closes."

Right. My focus has to be on JUSTICE FOR ROSALIE.

Two seconds later I turn around, and Dad's gone!

I swallow some sour panic juices trying to decide what to do: try to find him in this massive crowd, which is a complete needle in the haystack situation, and not get to the YMHA in time? Or go on my own? I remember how Dad showed me the route on the map. Hey, I may be just a kid from Kansas, but I've been on New York subways three times already this week. How hard can it be to get to 92nd and Lexington? If Dad can figure it out, so can I. Right?

CHAPTER 31
WEDNESDAY, JUNE 3

"**Y**ou've got what?" the YMHA receptionist asks. I could swear that's a wig she's wearing, lacquered down with a quart of hairspray.

"A locker key, real old." I keep watching for Dad. Bet he figured out I'd get to the YMHA by myself, and he's coming on the next subway.

The lady's palm's out. "Let's see the key."

"I don't exactly have it, but it's kind of important. Lives depend on it." Only a slight exaggeration. "Is there anybody who might know about old lockers? Like, what happened to stuff that was left in them thirty, forty years ago?" Then, to make it sound more official, I add, "My father's on his way," in case she thinks I'm just a kid playing a prank.

With a sigh, she jabs a prong into the switchboard and talks into the mouthpiece dangling over her lips. "Some *schmendrick's* here about an old key. You want to handle it, Izzy?"

A round-faced guy shuffles out. He's wearing a

yarmulke over a snarly nest of white curls and long curly earlocks, and he's about as old as Bubbie. Good sign.

"Sir, my Bubbie found an old key that's got this address on it. She's in Teaneck, New Jersey—"

"Mazel tov. Teaneck, very nice place."

"Yeah, I guess. So she needs me to claim my grandfather's stuff. He's been dead seven years."

"He should rest in peace. This way."

Izzy's office is about five feet square, with stacks of papers tacked helter-skelter to the walls and spilling out of file cabinets. An ancient black typewriter rules most of his desk, with a limp piece of paper hanging over the carriage.

Izzy eyes me suspiciously. "You're Jewish?"

Suddenly I'm defensive. Mr. Sokolov always makes me cover my head when we're studying Torah, but now . . . "Yeah, I'm Jewish. So?" Tough guy. Wish Dad would get here already.

"What was your zeyde's name?"

"Avrum Weitz, Abe. Do you remember him?" Like there aren't eight million people in New York, at least two million of 'em named Abe.

"I'm lousy with names. Not so good with faces, either." He goes to the farthest file cabinet and jerks open a drawer that's probably not seen daylight for thirty years. His fingers sift through fat folders. "Ah, here. Old history from before the flood." He looks at my blank face. "Noah and the big flood, way back. It's a joke, sonny. Give yourself a break. Smile a little."

"Sorry. I'm kind of in a hurry." And already worrying about how I'll get back to the hotel, since I blew all my money on the uptown subway.

"Weitz, Weitz," Izzy says. "Ahh!"

"You found something?"

"No, my back. I got a twinge." Finally he yanks out a piece of onionskin with a few faded lines typed on it. "Says here an Avram Weitz—*olev hashalom*, he should rest in peace—left a box in locker 347."

My heart leaps into my throat. "Can we go to the locker, sir?"

"At the junkyard? Those lockers came out of this building in 1948. Rusted from all the steam in the schvitz room. You should see the schmancy new ones. Rust-proof."

I squash my panic. "But what did you do with the leftover stuff?"

"This I happen to know about, sonny."

Clutching the bannister with both hands, he leads me down some marble stairs. Dad'll never find me down here in the catacombs. Izzy unlocks a door with one of the keys on a giant jangling ring looped through his belt. Inside the room is a random assortment of old junk piled on sagging shelves. Musty smells sting the inside of my nose.

"Your zeyde, he'd be in the W's, back here." Izzy huffs and puffs and turns tomato-red shifting boxes around. Sheesh, I hope he doesn't have a heart attack.

Things are tumbling out of the disintegrating cartons—grody socks, a pipe spraying tobacco. A rusted flashlight clatters to the cement floor. And there in the back I spot a metal strongbox with a label that says WEITZ. Yes!

"It's your lucky day, sonny. Where's the key?"

My spirit fizzes out as I shake my head.

"Didn't I say it was your lucky day, a nice grandson like you?" Izzy pulls a flat-blade screw driver from his key ring and jams it into the skinny space between the top and bottom of the strongbox. The old lock pops, and the lid springs open.

No million bucks inside, just official-looking papers and a faded, rumpled photo of an impossibly young Bubbie and Zeyde wearing Uncle Sam hats and waving little American flags. The picture's fastened by a rusted paper clip to a couple of bee-u-tee-ful citizenship certificates.

Upstairs, Dad's waiting for me and says, "Good thinking, Martin, well done." That's Dad's version of "WOWEEEEEE, kiddo! Ya hit it out of the park!"

CHAPTER 32
THURSDAY, JUNE 4

Day two of the hearing. We're wearing the same wrinkly, smelly outfits from yesterday, since we expected the whole thing to wind up in one day.

Groaning: "Aw, Mom, do I hafta wear the tie?"

"It's a full Windsor," Dad announces proudly as he ties the thing around my neck. A full Windsor must be another name for hangman's noose.

Mom's jamming her feet into those heels that look sharp enough to slice open a gut in the operating room. "Thanks to you and my mother, I might just beat this wrap. Where are the papers, Irwin?"

Dad waves a manila folder with copies of Bubbie and Zeyde's citizenship papers, dated 1907, plus their *ketubah*, the marriage contract, in the Jewish year 5660, which is 1906. Also a copy of Mom's birth certificate from 1909, and just to be sure, the official document proving that Zeyde was released from the Polish army nine years before Mom's birth. All that was in his strongbox, along with a note to Bubbie in his own handwriting:

Sylvie, listen, I don't trust nobody with these things, espe-cially not the fershtinkina goverment. Your loverboy, Avrum.

"My father was a character, all right." A bright smile smears across Mom's face, but she's crammed a lot more things into her overnight bag. When she catches me staring she says, "Might as well be comfortable and well-supplied in case I'm in stir a few weeks."

"Whoa, Mom, I thought the citizenship thing would be all you'd need."

"Oh, sure, Marty, it's just that we have to clear up the Mendelev matter, too. I don't believe he's dead. They said that to shock me. It's revolting how they've made a pawn of that fine gentleman." She locks her arms around me, as if I'm not already choking from the tie.

"Where are the papers?"

"Rosie, they're right here, I told you." Dad fans them across her face.

"Feels good." She puffs hair off her forehead. "Don't let them blow away, down the gutter."

◊

Vic joins Mom and Mr. Quincy at the witness table. A bunch of journalists and photographers doze in the back rows until things heat up, which happens about an hour into the questioning about Dr. Mendelev. These guys are really hung up on food. Again they want to know if he cooked *foreign* meals in our kitchen, like maybe he was baking commie propaganda in pirozhkis and blinis. And incidentally, he did cook these things for us, washed down by a lot of vodka, which they didn't let me guzzle.

Mom has the good sense to say he never cooked that stuff. A little lying under oath; what can it hurt? Ha!

Eventually they drop it, and one of the committee members says, "I have a few additional inquiries, Mrs. Rafner, regarding your status as a foreign national. You are, as I understand it, a citizen of Poland."

Our team is just waiting for this attack. Vic and Quincy both stand up, and Quincy holds the microphone right up to his mouth, making sure the reporters hear each word.

"As we speak, senators, the INS office here in Manhattan is reviewing a document providing indisputable evidence that Mrs. Rafner's parents, Sylvia and Avrum Weitz, became naturalized citizens of the United States in 1907, two years before the birth of their only child. That would be Rosalie Weitz Rafner, the witness who sits before you honorable gentlemen today."

Vic carries copies up to the senators, one pile for each, then sits down next to Mom. She's beaming.

This news ripples up and down the committee table, until one of the senators sputters, "When did this document *conveniently* turn up?"

By grabbing the mic, Mom signals Quincy and Vic that she doesn't need a pinch hitter. "Gentlemen, proof of my parents' citizenship vanished from the Chicago INS office under suspicious circumstances." She lets that sink in. "However, through excellent detective work on the part of my son, my parents' naturalization papers were found and have been delivered to the local INS office. Respectfully, senators, I must say that I'm as American as you are."

The old Rosalie is back in the game! Nobody says a word for a couple minutes as they eyeball the papers, and then the chairman says, "I understand you have your family with you today, Mrs. Rafner?"

"I do, yes, sir."

"How fortunate," the chairman drawls. "Would the members of Mrs. Rafner's family please rise?"

Firing squad? I kick the train case out of the way to get to my feet. My tie's flipped over, but I can't mess with it while everyone's watching, so I look like a nincompoop.

Next to me, Dad fumbles with his coat button, and his hat sails to the floor. Vic doesn't know whether to stand up or not, so he half rises, then drops down to his seat, emitting a whoopee-cushion noise. What a crew.

Mom stretches her arm toward Dad and me, grinning, showing lots of teeth. "My husband, Dr. Irwin Rafner, and our son, Martin Rafner." All the cameras spin toward us as the newsmen rush to the front of the hall. I'm blinded by flashbulbs. The whole world will see that I forgot to part my hair this morning.

The committee talks with their hands over their microphones, while we stand there like carnival ducks. Go on, toss the beanbag. An argument is brewing. Maybe somebody on the panel has the decency to know that they're giving Mom a bum deal.

The chairman clears his throat. "This subcommittee of the U.S. Senate does not wish to detain you further, Mrs. Rafner, while we peruse the *alleged* citizenship papers." With a sneer, he adds, "We have no desire to separate you from such a fine, upstanding family."

Yeah, we're still standing up.

"However, we reserve the right to recall you at some time in the future should we feel the need to pursue your questionable associations, specifically with the spy Mendelev. Dismissed."

Just like that, it's over. While the flashbulbs pop, making the room smell like it's about to catch fire, Vic comes over to us and whispers to me, "She's a tough babe, your mother."

My mother, a babe? Tough, yes. She's beat them at their own game. She hugs Quincy. Dad and I rush to her as the gavel pounds and the chairman bellows, "Next witness."

Before we're out of the hearing room, Mom pulls the bobby pins out of her knot and lets her hair tumble to her shoulders, like in real life.

We jackknife our way through a pack of journalists baiting her for some reaction.

"How ya feeling, Mrs. Rafner?"

"Relieved!"

"Excuse us, pardon me," Dad shouts, as we work our way through the crowd.

Another reporter nudges Dad with a mic. "What are your feelings today, Mr. Rafner?"

Mom spins around and says, "It's *Dr.* Rafner."

A mic is shoved half way up my nose. "So, where ya goin', Marvin?"

Dad breaks out in a wide beam, the best smile I've seen on him for ages. "It's *Martin*, for your information, and I'll answer that question. My wife, my son, and our legal team are going out in pursuit of the thickest, juiciest corned beef sandwich in the Lower East Side, after which we're heading home to Kansas."

Then some crackpot spoils the party by asking, "What're your thoughts two weeks before the Rosenberg execution?"

"No comment." Mom pushes the microphone out of the way and kicks off those stiletto heels. One hits the doorman, who takes it as a trophy, and the other lands in the sewer. We all get a charge out of seeing Mom run down the street in her stocking feet, with her hair flowing behind her. The seams up the back of her legs are all zigzaggy, but who cares?

We're free!

◊

On the train heading home, reality sets in. On some senator's whim, Mom could be called back. Even if she's not, who knows if she or Dad can stay at Hawthorne if she still refuses to sign the loyalty oath? We might have to move. Palmetto is home; always has been. I couldn't leave any more than Mickey Mantle could leave the Yankees.

Unless I have to.

As we're clackety-clacking along the train tracks, me tucked between the cool, crisp sheets of my bunk, my mind snaps to thoughts I've blotted out while I was focused on Mom's hearing. Mr. and Mrs. Rosenberg, these are their final fifteen days, unless there's a miracle like Bill Wambsganss's amazing unassisted triple play in the 1920 Series. He caught a line drive, stepped on Second for a put-out, then ran to First to tag out the batter.

Hey, miracles happen.

CHAPTER 33
THURSDAY, JUNE 11 –
SUNDAY, JUNE 14

Back in Palmetto, it's business as usual, except nothing is usual. You'd expect the FBI car to be gone, since Dr. Sonfelter's skipped town and Mom survived the SISS hearing, but no such luck. Guess Milgrim and Kluski haven't been told what their next gig is. News travels slow by carrier pigeon from D.C. to Kansas. Or else we're still under suspicion. After all, the SISS guys are looking over the citizenship papers, which they could *disappear* again, and they threatened to call Mom back any time. Maybe we'll never shake 'em.

I yank a rumpled shirt from the bottom of the laundry pile and run across the street to give Luke the signed Rizzuto card. He's back to sitting in his driveway. "Brought you something."

He takes the yellow envelope without a word and slides the beautiful 1949 Rizzuto card out of the cellophane pocket. Studies the autograph for about five long minutes. "This is . . . so fine . . . so very fine." He slips it in his shirt pocket, placing his hand over the pocket the way you do to sing "The Star-Spangled Banner."

Luke starts out so low and flat that I can barely hear him, and so slow that it's hard to connect the words.

"You . . . play . . . the . . . bugle . . . I . . . heard . . . you."

"Yeah, but I'm no good. We'll blow a few blasts at commencement, and that's it until next June."

"Don't . . . like . . . bugles . . . hundreds blaring . . . bitter-cold . . . night."

What's he talking about?

"Chosin . . . Reservoir." His eyes aren't dead now; they're thousands of miles away, back in Korea.

Word by drawn-out word: "You're hunched behind a hill. Can't feel your toes, but they're throbbing inside your stiff boots anyway. Chinese storm in on the side of the North. Bugles, that's their battle cry, bugles blaring, blaring. Supposed to unnerve the enemy, which is us, which is me. Shells bursting, lighting the black night. Blood, guts flying, and those bugles blaring, driving you 'round the bend. Head's splitting. Don't think you're going to get out alive. Lotta guys don't, your buddies don't, but you do. You do."

"Oh, man." What else can I say? A big sour wad clogs my throat. I'm about to either cry or puke.

Long silence, then, "Don't blow . . . the . . . bugle . . . anymore . . . Marty."

"I won't, Luke, I swear. Not at commencement, not anywhere. Ever."

Later, I stash the bugle in the back of my closet, under a sleeping bag, so there's no chance that I'll hear it blaring in the night, like Luke did at Chosin Reservoir.

◊

At the final bell, last day of school, a victory cry explodes all over the building. Guys are whooping it up and flinging notebook papers and gum wrappers and holey sneakers out of their lockers. Pirates toss their ball caps in the air and slug through the schoolyard like one big wobbly-celled amoeba, with Connor as the nucleus. You'd think they were a winning team, instead of the worst losers in Palmetto Junior-Senior High history. Makes me want to duck and cover again.

Well, who needs them? This is what I have going for me this summer:

- Luke Everly, who says three or four words a day that aren't about bugles
- the Mick, who hasn't got a clue that a guy named Marty Rafner even exists
- Mr. Sokolov and his *Read!*
- and the countdown to the Rosenbergs' execution next week.

How could it get any better than *that*—or worse?

Earthquake? No, Mom with her knee in my back, shaking me awake. "Wonderful news, Marty! Some new lawyers got a brief to the judge saying that the Rosenbergs were tried under the wrong law. Brand new evidence. There's hope!"

My head's foggy, and I stammer, "Does this mean they won't go to the Chair Thursday?"

"It might. Be happy for them, Marty!"

"I'm happy, I'm just not awake."

But by the time I am awake, the world's changed again. Mom's brushing her teeth at the kitchen sink. She turns around, foaming at the mouth with toothpaste, and mumbles, "The Supreme Court denied a stay of execution on a five to four vote."

"No hope?"

"Well, it's not over yet." She spits into the sink. "Those new lawyers are appearing before Justice Douglas for reconsideration. He's more open than the other three dissenters. At least the Rosenbergs might get a delay until October, because all the Supreme Court justices are leaving on vacation today. One's even scheduled for surgery, so there's no calling them back. October! Lots of things could happen to save them in four months. It's the only major victory the Rosenbergs have had in more than two years."

Good news, bad news, or is it worse news? It's hard

to tell. I need to escape. So I take a lawn chair across the street and park right next to Luke. I don't even try to make conversation. We just sit there like two geezers on the porch of the old folks' home.

Luke says, "I'm . . . going . . . away."

"Where ya going, Luke?"

"Can't . . . say."

"Wendy and Carrie, too?" Being a hopeless optimist, I stupidly want to believe they're all heading to the lake together for a little sun.

"It's . . . not . . . your . . . fault."

"What's not?"

"You . . . did your . . . best . . . kid. Go . . . home."

◊

The radio's blasting some cheerful Perry Como number when I walk back inside. Mom grabs me and plants her hand on my shoulder and plasters her palms to my sweaty ones. "We need a little cheering up. It's in honor of Ethel Rosenberg. She'll never be able to foxtrot with her sons."

Mom guides me around the room, since I can't dance worth spit, but before I know it, she's swinging me this way and that, pumping my arm, twirling under my armpit like I'm a giant and she's four feet tall. My feet move—everything moves, including my liver and spleen—in time to Perry Como warbling, *"Don't let the stars get in your eyes, don't let the moon break your hearrr-art . . ."*

CHAPTER 34
WEDNESDAY, JUNE 17

One day left for the Rosenbergs. I picture them in their individual cells poring over their lists of things they wanted to get done before their lives went dark forever: Climb Mount Everest, eat kangaroo steak in Tasmania, learn to play pinochle, take in a World Series game, see your sons old enough to shave.

The radio's reporting last night's ball scores, interrupted by news.

". . . a late-breaking bulletin in the Rosenberg case: Chief Justice Vinson has ordered the Supreme Court justices to return to Washington for an unprecedented special session to review Justice Douglas's stay of execution, issued earlier today. Justice Black, scheduled for surgery this week, has delayed his operation and will meet with his brethren on the Court."

Good news!

". . . expected that the Court will vacate Justice Douglas's stay, and that the execution will be carried out on Friday, June 19, at 11:00 p.m. Stay tuned for further developments."

Bad news.

Yesterday it was two days to go. Now, a day later, it's still two days to go. Weird math. It would confuse even Dr. Sonfelter. Does it count as good news if you got yourself ready to die on a certain day, then it got bumped back?

Mom's sitting at the kitchen table with her head propped up in her hands. "Don't say anything, Marty. I need to figure out how I feel." She passes me the *Sentinel*. There it is on the front page:

ROBBY AND MICHAEL VISIT
PARENTS FOR LAST TIME

They'll never see their mom and dad again, so I'm trying to figure out what they'll talk about in the reception room at Sing Sing.

SON 1: So long. It's been a nice few years, except for the last two while you've been in jail and we've been farmed out to anybody who'd take us.

PARENT 1: Have a good life.

PARENT 2: Sorry we'll miss the next seventy years of it.

SON 2: *Hope it doesn't hurt too much when they pull the switch. Hey, he kicked me!*

SON 1: *Did not!*

SON 2: *Did too!*

PARENT 1: *Boys, boys, no fighting.*

PARENT 2: *Always remember, sons, we love you.*

SON 1: *Yeah? Funny way of showing it.*

Maybe it won't be like that at all. Maybe they'll be slobbering and hugging and promising things that can't ever happen. I'll always be with you. Or maybe they'll just find ways to hang out in different corners of the boxing ring.

The whole Rosenberg thing is making me sick, which means hungry. I slap two pieces of bread and a chunk of Velveeta into a pan. So, while I'm waiting for it to get gooey, there's a shadowy shape outside the kitchen door—someone's head, but I can't tell whose because of the checkered curtains on the window. An envelope slides under the door, and the shadow disappears.

Another threatening note? I thought we were past that. I pick up the yellow envelope with my heart pounding.

Inside is the Phil Rizzuto card; no note. Why is Luke returning it to me?

I stand there for a long time, trying to puzzle it out, until smoke and the nasty smell of burning cheese shakes me into action. Turn off the stove and fly out the kitchen door, still clutching the yellow envelope. I sprint across the street without looking for traffic. The FBI guys will honk if a car comes barreling down Oxbow. They wouldn't want me splattered on their windshield.

A gust of wind has blown Luke's chair across his lawn because he isn't there to anchor it. I ring the bell, knock, look in all the windows, the backyard. The garage door won't go up, and all the doors are locked, no lights on anywhere. Where'd he go? And why did he return the card that he'd called *so very fine*?

At the FBI car: "You know the guy who's always sitting right there outside his garage except when he rolled down the driveway? Did you see him leave?"

"We didn't see a thing," Kluski replies. Some spies *they* are.

But Milgrim, who still has a human bone left in his body, says, "Correction: he walked north, up toward the campus."

I run to the College, with my two keys flopping on a chain against my T-shirt. It's a big campus with lots of buildings and trees and cars. How can I zero in on him? As soon as I clear one place, he can move into it after me.

I mean, like he's experienced in combat, boondoggling the enemy.

If I were running away, where would I go? Up to Whittier Tower, where I'm emperor of the world, because I'm the only one besides Connor's father who has a key.

Unless Luke made himself a copy that day he made my house key! Yeah, the tower key was on the same string. He even commented on it.

I swear, it takes me less than a minute to sprint to Whittier. The door's so tall that I have to stand on my toes to reach the lock with the key around my neck.

It's already unlocked.

The stubborn door creaks open onto darkness, and I start climbing up the winding stairs, quiet as an alley cat. They say that when you're in a scary situation adrenaline pumps through you. That's how an ordinary kid can lift the front end of a car, or run the mile in four. Me, I never dreamed I'd have the energy to climb these stairs so fast, no gasping.

All the way up the corkscrew stairs I'm thinking about what to say. Nothing seems right. Should I pull a Mom and ask him a zillion questions? No, no questions. Should I lie? *I just happened to be on my way up here; thought I'd keep you company.* Talk about dumb. Guilt, will that work? Some Bubbie Sylvia psychology? *I'm really disappointed in you, Luke. If you fall, you'll smash the pretty flowers down there. Now, that's not a nice thing to do, is it, sweetheart?*

Should I beg him to come down with me? Should I grab him and wrestle him to the floor? Sure, like he isn't three times bigger and stronger than I am. But there are those war wounds; maybe I can take him.

Nothing feels right. I'm a kid. I'm not trained to do stuff like this. But maybe he just wants company while he enjoys the breeze on a hot, humid day. Yeah, that's it.

I'm panting my way up the last ten steps when I remember him saying, *It's not your fault . . . You did your best, kid.* Sure sounds like goodbye.

CHAPTER 35
WEDNESDAY, JUNE 17

My lungs feel like water balloons by the time I see light at the top of the stairs. I don't want to scare Luke. So, before he hears my footsteps getting closer, I call out in a real calm voice, "Hey, Luke, it's me, Marty. How ya doing?" I wait to see if he'll answer. "I brought you your Phil Rizzuto. You didn't mean to give it back to me, did you? He signed it to you." Probably wrecked a $15 card by sticking it in my back pocket, but that's not my main worry right now.

I'm on the third step from the top, just high enough that my head shows over the platform. Already there's enough wind that my hair whips around my face. He better be holding on tight. Don't see him, but he's nearby; I feel him there, like heavy air. I slide the envelope across the floor, as far as I can reach, anchoring it with my fist.

"I forgot to check the lineup for tonight's game, Luke. Don't know if Rizzuto's playing, but I'd sure like to get down to my radio in time for the first pitch, wouldn't you?"

Ahead of me, wind and Luke. Behind me, dark winding stairs that look real inviting all of a sudden. But I'm in too deep to turn back.

I'm up on the platform now, but not too close to him. Just crouching there on my knees, catching my breath, hunched up against the stone wall. The bell blocks my view of the other side of the tower; the bell-pull is close enough that I could yank it, and it would cause a thundering clang, turning us stone-deaf for life.

"Hey, Luke? You heard, didn't ya, that the Army drafted Willie Mays?"

No comment.

"Aren't you wondering what the Giants are gonna do without Mays for two whole seasons?"

Is Luke listening? The wind dies down a little. Now his breathing is the only sound. So silent up here, so peaceful. So treacherous. "Anyway, it's not gonna be Yankees-Giants this year in the Series. Wanna make a bet it's gonna be Yankees-Dodgers?" I inch like a crab along the wall.

Now I see his Marine boots, polished to a blinding shine. "Luke? What do you think? Yankees, for sure, right? You said it yourself, Rizzuto all the way." I keep scooting along on my rear, pushing the yellow envelope ahead of me.

Suddenly his boot comes down on the envelope, sending my heart hammering. Blood rushes through my veins like they're hot water pipes. He's in full white dress uniform, Marines cap and all. He stands ramrod-straight, with his back to me.

"Who . . . sent . . . you . . . up . . . here, kid?"

"Nobody. You knew I had a key, you cut it yourself. Made yourself one, too. So, I guess we're both s'posed to be up here. It's kind of cozy, don't you think?"

Cozy? It's terrifying, and I'm three parts chicken, even on the ground.

Suddenly Luke bends over the half-wall like he's trying to pick up a nickel on the ground, three hundred feet down.

"Hey, man, don't do that! Want me to have a heart attack?"

He raises his head, his chest, in slow motion, then snaps back into attention, gloved hands clasped behind his back. Phew! Close call. It must hurt his war wounds to stand so rigid. Seems like he's not moving a muscle or taking a breath, like he's sealed in ice.

The wind stirs up again, enough to make the bell swing a little. Its rusty chain creaks, which makes my skin crawl. Now he stands in the open space, holding on to nothing but air and swaying like the bell. If his Marines cap weren't strapped under his chin, it would fly to the next county. His pants legs flap in the wind. The wind could knock him right over the edge!

I huddle against the wall of the tower, hoping my cold sweat will glue me to the stone. "Listen, it's a little windy up here, Luke, and the radio says a storm's on its way." A lie, but I've got to use whatever ammunition I can muster up. "I don't know about you, but it's scaring me, 'cause everybody knows I'm a sniveling coward."

Here's his chance to agree. Nothing.

"So, would you mind if we both went on down the stairs?"

I watch him unsnap his cap and slip it off his head. His buzz cut is too short to catch the breeze as he flings that cap down, way off across the next building.

"Say, I was just thinking about Carrie. Cute kid. What happens when she's old enough to swing a bat? Which one of us is gonna be her coach, you or me?"

He doesn't take the bait.

"Better be you, because I swing at everything, even a goose egg. Hey, I'd swing at a watermelon. I'll bet Carrie's got natural talent. You think your daughter's got what it takes to be a lady jock when she gets bigger?"

No answer but the howling wind.

Deep breath: "Listen, I've got the number to reach Wendy. I'm gonna tell her to bring Carrie over here. I want to see for myself if she's got quick reflexes, you know? See if there's any hope for her to be the best slugger on our block someday."

He still stands there swaying. His lips move like he's saying a prayer. This is crazy. We've gotta get down those stairs, both of us. My heart thumps so hard it feels like it's swelled to fit my whole chest and is beating against my bones to escape.

Quick, I need a new plan. Last ditch effort. It's a gamble, but nothing else has worked.

"Okay, here's the deal, Luke. I'm starting down, 'cause, I'm getting a little panicky up here in this wind, and I don't like the way that bell's starting to swing. So, I'm going to yell out one-to-ten slowly as my foot hits each step, okay? By the time I get to ten, you'll be on the first step, heading down. Do we have a deal?"

Luke moves his boot and bends over to pick up the Rizzuto envelope, which he sticks inside his coat. Is this a good sign?

I swallow dry. "Do we have a deal?" I start down the cobbled, winding steps. The dungeon wall oozes fuzzy slime, but I cling to it like a barnacle to a boat.

Shouting behind me: "One. Two. Do we have a deal, Luke? Do we? Three. I can't hear you. Four."

He's not coming. Is he gonna stay up there until it gets dark? All night? Forever?

"Five . . . Say something, Luke, I'm getting pretty shook up. Do we have a deal or don't we?" Long pause. "Six . . . seven . . . eight."

What am I supposed to do? Should I be praying? What would Mr. Sokolov do? There are Jewish prayers for everything, like one to thank God for making the rooster able to tell whether it's day or night. Who thinks up this stuff? There's even one for when you take a leak, so there's got to be some kind of a prayer for this situation. Where's Mr. Sokolov when I really need him?

Maybe I should have counted in Hebrew; slower, more syllables. *Ehad, shtaim, shalosh . . .*

"Can't hear you, Luke. Nine!" I shout. "Nine and a half . . . Nine and two thirds . . . Nine and three quarters." I scramble down a few more steps and wait.

"Deal," Luke says faintly.

Did I hear it, or just imagine it?

And here comes his boot on the first step, and his voice saying, "One . . . two . . . three . . . " real slow and steady.

I'm dizzy with relief and take a deep breath so I don't tumble head over heels to the bottom.

Luke and I count all the way down, four hundred and sixteen winding stone steps, to the oaken door. I walk out ahead of him, squinting in the bright sunlight, and I'm surprised to see a circle of spectators who must have spotted us up there and followed the silent drama.

"Stand back," I shout as Luke comes out that door and marches in lock-step, a proud U.S. Marine. The small crowd parts for him, and soon it's just Luke and me, across campus and down Oxbow Road, right to my front door.

No speeches, no music, no floats with paper flowers, no signs and banners, but it's a parade for a genuine hero, the parade Corporal Luke Everly earned over there surviving the icy night of the bugles.

CHAPTER 36
WEDNESDAY, JUNE 17 – THURSDAY, JUNE 18

People are saying I'm some big hero. Amy Lynn believes I absolutely saved Luke's life. Even Milgrim said, "Good job, kid."

I don't feel like a life-saver or a hero, and what's a hero anyway? Somebody caught in a bad situation who's lucky enough to try something that works.

I'm just glad Luke's on solid ground. Wendy and Carrie came and got him. They're all with Wendy's parents in Newton. The Marines are getting him shrink help. He'll be okay. He's got Rizzuto in his pocket.

◊

We're on our way back from a "Clemency for the Rosenbergs" rally in Wichita. Mom says, "It's a violation of everything American. No one's ever been executed for espionage in this country, much less a husband and wife leaving behind two little boys. And on such sketchy evidence."

I've heard it all a zillion times.

"Those folks who want blood, don't they realize this death makes martyrs of the Rosenbergs?" Dad asks. "Guilty or innocent, their case will echo for generations. Mark my words, Rosalie, long after we're dead and buried, people will still be talking about Julius and Ethel Rosenberg."

Mom sighs. "So, all we can do is wait and see whether Eisenhower will grant presidential clemency. If that letter Ethel wrote him doesn't defrost his heart, he's not human. It just has to reach him in the next few hours. All he has to do is raise one eyebrow, sign a paper, and the nightmare is over, for good."

But it's *not* over.

Today Mr. Rosenberg had his last visit with his brother and sister and mother. Mom and Dad are hashing it over in the front seat.

Mom turns around to face me. "What can a mother say to her son two days before he's to be executed? I hope to God I don't survive you, Marty. That would kill me."

"I better not ever be facing the electric chair." It's gloom and doom in the DeSoto. Hope hangs by a hair on the Supreme Court's last-ditch decision, and on Ike. Roller coaster; we don't know how to feel as we turn the corner onto Oxbow Road—where our house is lit up like a carnival.

"I didn't leave lights on, did you, Rosalie?"

"Oh, good grief, it's my mother. She's the only one who throws every window open, rain or shine."

Sure enough, Bubbie Sylvia has commandeered our kitchen and greets us with a wooden spoon dripping soup. After hugs and kisses, she pinches my cheeks. "Look at you, sweetheart. Not a pimple on your gawgeous face."

Mom groans. "What are you doing here, Ma? It's a long way from New Jersey."

"Listen, I know what tomorrow is. Julius and Ethel." She leans forward, though she doesn't have far to go, this little woman Connor calls the Human Fireplug. "Today's their fourteenth wedding anniversary, yet. Oy. So, you shouldn't be alone at a terrible time like tomorrow, and a little turkey barley soup can't hurt. I brought the turkey bones on the aeroplane, such an aroma! Here, taste. Delicious, didn't I tell you?"

Dad asks, "Did you think about calling first, Sylvia?"

"Long-distance? Of course not!" Bubbie rescues a carrot from the soup pot and charges toward me with the spear. "Tell me, is it too mushy? Never mind, I don't want to know. Tell me instead, you got everything worked out at the College?"

Mom sighs, and Dad rescues her. "The good news is the Hawthorne board voted on Tuesday to ban all faculty loyalty oaths, in keeping with Quaker religious principles. They admit they should have done it years ago. They were trying to adapt to the political climate."

"So, Rosalie, you're back teaching that poetry nonsense?"

"Not so simple, Ma. The board went over the case against me, including a transcript of the hearing in New York. They've asked me to resign. I'm a liability." Mom snorts. "A liability! I'm the conscience of the College."

"Oy, you're as stubborn as your father, may my Avrum rest in peace."

"I've been offered a teaching position over at Bethel College in Newton. Mennonites, they're open-minded. And with only two classes, I'll have time for my own poetry *nonsense*."

Yeah, like I've had all that free time since I was booted off the Pirates. At least Mom's not moving us to the Deep South. Though Dad does keep reminding us that a lot of fine Negro colleges are thrilled to get Ph.D. profs even if they've fallen under the evil eye of the Carnivore.

"She could be called back before the SISS committee any time, Sylvia, but, at least we're not facing deportation to Poland, thanks to your excellent record-keeping," Dad teases.

"Poland, ach, you wouldn't want to live there these days. Such a shortage of meat, and the winters, don't ask."

Connor taps at our kitchen door, his mug framed in the window.

"Oh, it's that nice little boy you play with!" Bubbie says.

If she hadn't been there, I might've opened the door just so I could slam it in Connor's face, but instead I rush outside.

Connor's got a basketball on his hip. "I heard about Luke Everly and the tower yesterday. Musta been pretty nerve-wracking."

"Yeah, you know what it's like up there." After that we don't know what to say to each other, with Bubbie mugging at us out the window. We shift from foot to foot until, idiot that I am, I start singing the *Dragnet* theme song, *Dum da-dum dum; dum da-dum dum, DUM!* Connor picks up on it and fakes Jack Webb's deep, rolling voice: "The facts, ma'am, just the facts."

It's a start that I'm not sure I want.

CHAPTER 37
FRIDAY, JUNE 19

My stomach's churning this morning, like after I've eaten a whole row of Oreos dunked in milk. This time it's not about anything I've snarfed down. It's about *them*, the Rosenbergs. This is the day, one day late.

I collapse onto a chair at the kitchen table. The radio's tuned low, and the announcer reports on the huge crowd flashing signs: *JUSTICE AND MERCY* and *DON'T MURDER THE ROSENBERGS*. Then comes the daily on-again-off-again ride. Since the Supreme Court has refused to uphold Justice Douglas's stay of execution, it's *on* for tonight, eleven p.m. Only a few more hours to sweat it out for Mr. and Mrs. Rosenberg and all the rest of us.

Bubbie says, "At least they didn't die on their wedding anniversary. Wait, eleven o'clock? After sundown. They're going to assassinate two Jews on our Sabbath? I don't believe it!"

Mom jumps up to grab her avocado-pit plant with its two pathetic limp leaves, and she suddenly yanks it out of the mayo jar, rips out the life-support toothpick holders, and tosses the whole thing into the waste basket.

"Ah, that feels better." She stomps out of the kitchen.

Bubbie dips a spoon into some goo in a bowl and waves it at me. "Taste. It needs a little cinnamon?" She puts down the spoon and runs her fingers through her curly, bluish hair. "Tell me, sweetheart, is your mother all right?"

"Mom's a rock," I assure her. "You should have seen her at the SISS hearing. She had those senators shaking with fear."

"Yes, but the College gave her such a clop, and tonight . . ." We both know what tonight means. "On Shabbos. How could they?"

"Aw, Mom will probably write five prize-winning poems about the whole deal."

"And you, sweet boy? How are you doing?"

I'm startled, because suddenly I realize that nobody has asked me that since Whittier Tower. Mom, Dad, Connor, the Marines, Wendy—they're all caught up in their own stuff, and the Rosenberg thing is so gargantuan. Me, I'm just the kid hanging around burning grilled cheese and getting kicked off the baseball team.

"Wanna go for a walk, Bubbie?"

Down the street, I pour all of it out—my hurt over the Pirates and Coach Earlywine and Connor, and how scary it is to think about somebody's mom and dad getting killed tonight, *legally*.

Bubbie slips in a bunch of *oohs* and *oys*.

"Can I ask you something? Are my parents as weird as I think they are?"

"Yes, but they're like a terrible pair of pajamas with fire engines. Wait a while, and you'll outgrow them."

"It's not fair, Bubbie." Like the Rosenbergs, and the way the senators cut Mom off when she had something important to say, and Dr. Sonfelter hiding out who-knows-where, and Luke locked inside his own head. *Hey, that's life*, Connor used to say about stuff like that. That shouldn't be *life*.

Bubbie draws herself up to her full four-foot-ten and says, "You're telling *me* things aren't fair? Did I expect to be a widow, alone in my golden years?"

Near the FBI car Milgrim's checking her out. They've probably got a thick file on her already.

"Hello, gentlemen! You should get out, get a little exercise like my grandson and me."

Milgrim answers, "We'll consider that, ma'am. It's a balmy day."

After we're past them, Bubbie asks, "Who are those bums loitering there?"

"FBI spies. They watch every move we make."

"What, they don't have criminals to go after?" Bubbie has trouble catching her breath and her ankles hang over her shoes like bread dough.

"You and Zeyde, back when you were young, did you think about things the same way Mom does?"

"Sweetheart, seventy-six years I'm living, and I never met *anybody* who thinks the way your mother does, except almost my Avrum, he should rest in peace. But a finer mensch you never met. You know the Yiddish word, *mensch*? It means not just a man, but a person with character, backbone, heart. My Avrum had it all, and not bad looking, on top of it."

"He was your loverboy."

Bubbie blushes. "If you only knew!"

"I don't want to know." I think for a second. "I guess Mom's a real mensch."

"The best kind, but sometimes I could scream from her, just like her father. It isn't easy, is it?"

We reach the corner at Oxbow and Greenwich. "Want to turn back?" I ask.

Bubbie does a little jig. "Once more around the dance floor, sweet boy. I need the exercise to keep my girlish figure," says the Human Fireplug.

CHAPTER 38

FRIDAY, JUNE 19

Definitely. Tonight. There's only one thing that can stop them throwing the switch. President Eisenhower has to suddenly get a conscience. He should have one; he's a Kansan, from right over there in Abilene. But he's already said no once, and now there's that letter Mrs. Rosenberg wrote that begs him to reconsider. It might not even get to him in time, because they've moved up the eleven o'clock execution.

After thousands of people all over the world protested about killing Jews on their Sabbath, the prison guys are making a big concession. Since Shabbos begins at sundown, and sundown isn't until eight-thirty in New York, they'll do the deed at eight. It'll be history by sundown. Man, they're all heart.

Here's what gets me: the warden's scared that Mr. Rosenberg will try to commit suicide. What—take all the fun away from the Sing Sing executioner? What a way to make a living. So, they stripped everything out of Julius Rosenberg's cell, even his insect collection.

Guess they thought he could kill himself by swallowing dried cockroaches. Man, that's a fate worse than death.

Mom knocks on my bedroom door. "There's a vigil at Bethel College. Want to go with Dad and me? It's important for solidarity, so the Rosenbergs know the world cares."

Do I want to go? No, because it's hopeless. It won't change a thing. They're still going to the Chair tonight, no matter what some kid in Kansas does. But I think about the Rosenberg People on the train, and the thousands demonstrating on the streets of New York, and . . . and . . .

"Yeah, I wanna go with you."

So we join the quiet crowd at noon. No speeches, no chants, no signs waving at the sun and clouds. Just three hundred sad people with arms locked, in silent respect, because in a few hours, like distant stars, two humans will wink out forever.

What do people do when they know they only have a few hours to live? I hear Julius and Ethel will be spending the afternoon together, facing each other on chairs, with a mesh screen between them. Maybe they can bump knees and kiss goodbye through mesh holes. Will they walk together down that cinderblock hall, holding icy hands?

After the vigil, shadows are getting longer. Amy Lynn and I sit on my front porch steps.

"I wonder how Luke's doing with his family in Newton. You saved his life, Marty, you did," Amy Lynn says again.

"Not really. I don't think he was really gonna jump or anything. He just needed to be up there. It's powerful." I don't tell her I go up there for the same reason. Now it seems unreal, what happened up there with Luke two days ago.

Amy Lynn grabs my hand in both of hers; tears fill her eyes. "I've been to see my father. Shh, don't say a word. I'm not supposed to tell you. End of subject, okay?"

"My lips are zipped." If I squint, I can just see the position of the hands on the tower clock. Five-fifteen. Six-fifteen in New York. "In two hours it'll be over."

"Ethel sings to him through the cold stone walls, Marty, and he writes letters to her and calls her *my sunshine*. It's so utterly tragic, just like Heloise and Abelard."

"I hope it turned out better for them than it's gonna for Ethel and Julius."

"It didn't." Amy Lynn gives me back my sweaty hand. "I think I'll know, I'll feel it, the minute they pull the switch, don't you think you will?"

"Probably." Six-thirty. Time for their last meal. In the movies, the Death Row cons always order a T-bone steak and French fries, with strawberry shortcake for dessert. Wonder what the Rosenbergs picked to eat on both sides of the mesh screen. And what Rabbi Koslowe will say to them. He's the only one who's allowed to visit them in these final hours.

"I better go home and sit with my mother. She can't face this alone." Amy Lynn slides down the steps and jumps to her feet. "I'll see you . . . afterward."

◊

We listen to the countdown on the radio. I'm doodling, and Dad's randomly filling in crossword squares. Passing time.

Mom viciously tears a head of lettuce into shreds. "Do you realize that this is the first daylight execution in the history of Sing Sing? They usually cover their shame with darkness."

Doodle. Doodle. "I hope Robby and Michael are asleep before eight o'clock."

The radio drones in the center of the kitchen table. We're eager for news, bulletins, hope. We wait to hear if Eisenhower will be won over by Mrs. Rosenberg's personal letter to him. They keep quoting one line: *I ask this man, whose name is one with glory, what glory there is that is greater than the offering to God of a simple act of compassion!*

Mrs. Rosenberg is really laying it on thick, but hey, the stakes are pretty high. Maybe President Eisenhower isn't just a war hero. Maybe he's a mensch. He's still got an hour to make up his mind.

Mom sometimes forgets to light candles on Friday night, but not Bubbie. So, on the counter next to the toaster are the Shabbos candles they'll be lighting and blessing just before sundown, which is at seven-twenty-three here. By the time it's sundown for us in Kansas, they'll already be dead. Unless Ike comes through.

Mom turns up the volume. "Shh! Another announcement!"

CHAPTER 39
FRIDAY, JUNE 19

The reporter's voice shakes as he reads the late-breaking bulletin: "It appears that Julius and Ethel Rosenberg have reached the end of their appeal process in the eleventh hour before their execution, as moments ago the office of President Dwight Eisenhower issued this statement: 'The President has read the letter of the defendant Ethel Rosenberg. He states that in his conviction it adds nothing to the issues covered in his statement of this afternoon.'"

Mom slams the table, sending the napkins flying out of the holder. The giraffe salt shaker falls on his nose. "I'm ashamed for the whole country. It's a mockery of our judicial system. Shame, shame, shame." She clicks off the radio. "I don't want to hear a blow-by-blow when they march them down to the death chamber."

I still haven't shaken off the gloom of this afternoon's silent vigil, mixed with the sad conversation with Amy Lynn. And now that sad feeling morphs again, and I'm pumped full of a rage so wide and deep that I want to tear down the checkered curtains, hurl the toaster out the window, pull up floor boards with my bare hands. I want to race up to school and grab Coach Earlywine by the neck and . . .

I gotta get out of the house and flex some muscles or I'll explode like a bomb. That's creepy, since the Rosenberg's are dying because of A-bomb secrets.

A basketball has rolled down the driveway and is lodged in the wet gutter next to the FBI car. Milgrim and Kluski are listening to the countdown on their car radio. I toe the dripping ball up into my hands. My shots leave the rim shaking violently, hit or miss. This one for the judge who sentenced them. This shot for Truman, who denied clemency last year. One for Ike, who said no twice today. Another one for the Sing Sing guy who'll be tripping the switch. I'm breathing like I've run a mile, panting, gasping for air between shots, then firing that ball like I could *kill* the goal. Kill it.

I sense someone coming up behind me, but I don't turn around because I'm planning to blindside whoever it is by ramming that ball at him until his guts spill. I hope it's Milgrim. Kluski would be my second choice.

But it's Connor. "You're missing three out of every four."

"So? Can you do better?" I jam the ball into his roll of fat. His arms close around it. He stretches, lines up, eyes the rim, positions his feet, toes the line, flexes his shooting arm, rolls his shoulders, dribbles three times, eyeballs the goal again, takes a deep breath, shoots—and falls short of the basket by a foot.

"Out of practice," Connor mutters.

"Gimme the ball." Suddenly I'm hot. It doesn't matter where I stand, how far I am from the goal. I just keep hurling that ball up toward the basket like it's magnetized, and every shot sinks, *whoosh*, without even banking off the backboard. That old adrenaline thing, I guess.

I mutter, "You know what's happening, probably right now?"

"Julius and Ethel, yeah."

We don't talk for a while. We dribble and shoot, him missing more than he sinks.

Connor says, "Too bad about the Pirates finishing in last place in the league."

"Tell me something I don't already know."

"Okay, *this*. Where's my head been since the whole commie thing started? I'm real sorry I've been such a jerk."

Slam against the backboard. *Whoosh*, practically ripping the net. "Jerk doesn't cover it. And you know what? You've got no arm, so why did Coach play you at short? You're sure no Phil Rizzuto."

"Wait. That's hittin' below the belt." Connor intercepts the ball and bounces it, then hugs it to his chest. "It's just the times, Marty, all that Cold War yak and everybody seeing red, you know?"

"I *don't* know. Anyway, we had lots of years before all this stuff started happening."

"That's what I've been thinking. Remember the Kansas City road trip to see Mickey Mantle? You and me and my dad talking baseball two hundred miles each way?"

I tuck the ball under my arm, wiping sweat on the shoulder of my T-shirt. "Get this straight, Connor. I wouldn't even go to a dog fight with your father."

"Hey, whaddaya got against my old man?"

I hear the telephone voice in my head again: *Pack up quick and ride that Red Rail right out of town . . .*

"Nothin,' Connor. Nothin' I can prove."

"What's that s'posed to mean?" He starts dribbling the ball in a tight circle. "He's my only dad. What can I do? Your dad's not such a bargain, either."

I snatch the ball away from him and kick it from foot to foot, like the Harlem Globetrotters. I want to say, *Lay off my father, he's a real decent guy,* but I think about his question and before I know it, the words are out of my mouth. "Here's what you can do. Turn out different."

Another impressive *whoosh,* this one for Michael Rosenberg.

He waits a long time before answering. "I sort of get what you're saying, Marty."

Whoosh, one for Robert Rosenberg.

Connor says, "You hear about the Red Sox-Tigers game yesterday? World records, man. Seventh inning, Boston sends up twenty-three batters, and seventeen of 'em score runs. Sammy White gets three himself. Fourteen hits, and that rookie outfielder, Gene Stephens? He ends up the only American League guy to get three hits in the same inning. Red Sox trounce Detroit twenty-three to three."

"If it's not the Yankees, and Mantle's not playing, I'm not interested." I'm not giving Connor a drop of satisfaction, although I'm pretty snowed by the stats on that game. I hurl the ball into Connor's belly. "Shoot!" I growl through clenched teeth.

He shoots and misses.

I grab it on the rebound and dribble up and down the driveway like Luke used to do, and bag an amazing shot from this side of Milgrim and Kluski. Sends the rim boing-ing like it's been knocked out in a fight. Kluski nearly falls out of the car admiring that maneuver.

A few more shots. We're both bagging them left and right.

Then he goes and breaks the charm. "So, uh, about commencement next year. I'm thinking we oughta blow our bugles together, like we used to. Sounded dumb doing it alone this year."

"Nope, no more bugle-blowing for me, Connor. Luke and I had a big talk about it."

He shrugs his shoulders, trying to figure it out, but I'm not giving him any more clues. Too personal, the stuff Luke told me. Man, I still can't believe he trusted me up on that tower. Was it thinking about his family, about Wendy, and about Carrie growing up without him, that gave Luke the courage to follow me down those zillion steps to face the stuff that's haunting him? Man, if he could do that, anybody could.

Something catches my eye, something shimmery in the window, backlit behind the checkered curtains. I make out the fireplug form of Bubbie and Mom and Dad flanking her. Bubbie has a handkerchief covering her hair. Her hands are cupped over two flickering candles. She gathers the flame toward her. Her lips and Mom's move with the prayer.

Nearly sundown here. It's all over, *there*.

Robby and Michael. Wonder what it feels like to go to sleep having parents, and wake up as the most famous orphans in America? I don't ever want to know.

Connor looks at his watch. "It's done, isn't it?"

All I can do is nod.

"I guess things change, huh?"

Man, do they ever. I pass the ball to him with more style than vengeance, and when he rushes forward to catch it, his Pirates ball cap flies off and lands in a gutter puddle.

"Aw, man!" he bellows, and I laugh till my stomach aches and I feel a little of the anger hissing out of me.

Afterward, dripping with sweat, we turn on the hose for a drink, and he says, "Buddies?"

"Not so quick."

"Maybe next week?"

"I'll let you know."

CHAPTER 40
SUNDAY, JUNE 21

So, if I were gonna write one of those old memos to Mantle, which you can bet I'm not, here's what it would say:

From the desk of
IRWIN RAFNER, Ph.D.'s son Marty

DATE: June 21, 1953

TO: Mickey Mantle

It's done, Mick. All over Friday, by 8:17 Eastern. What's left to talk about? Just baseball, I guess. So, it's gonna be Yankees-Dodgers again, right? I gotta figure out a way to miss school so I can watch the Series on television. Hope it'll go the full seven. I'm going to watch with Luke Everly. Maybe Connor'll watch with us, too, since we're sort of friends again.

So, I'm planning to come down with elephantiasis or Guinea worm disease just in time for Game One. I've got from now till October to figure out how to catch it. Call me if you have any ideas. The FBI guys would be thrilled to hear your voice. They're still out there.

Your friend,
MARTY

AUTHOR'S NOTE

Cold War—it's an oxymoron, like *jumbo shrimp* and *good grief.* Yet it describes the intense post–World War II rivalry between two superpowers, the communist Soviet Union and the democratic/capitalist United States. No shots are fired between the two opposing nations, but salvos are lobbed in the form of accusations and atomic bomb threats.

So, what is capitalism? It's a system based on private property, including private control of factories and businesses, aimed at the accumulation of wealth and goods. A capitalist system is controlled by a free, competitive market, not by the workers or the government. While capitalism often goes hand in hand with democracy, it tends to create a society of *haves* and *have-nots*, of poverty in the midst of plenty.

Well, then, is a communistic society better? The original concept of communism is that all power, ownership, and production of goods should be in the hands of the people, the workers. Government would barely be needed. There would be no private ownership of land or goods, no class distinctions among people, and no *haves* and *have-nots*. The idea is, *from each according to his ability, to each according to his needs*. Though it sounds ideal, in practice communist governments have ripped power and freedom away from the people and have turned into repressive dictatorships, controlling every aspect of their citizens' lives.

In June 1950, a hot war flares when communist-supported North Korea attacks its southern neighbor, the Republic of Korea. America sends in troops to support the South Koreans, and by the time a truce is called three years later, 54,000 U.S. soldiers lie buried, and another 100,000 return wounded in body, mind, and spirit.

At home, Americans rally to protect democracy by weeding out any hint of communist influence. What a perfect opportunity for Wisconsin's Senator Joseph McCarthy to claim inside information on communists in the State Department, the CIA, universities, and the U.S. Army. FBI Director J. Edgar Hoover is already waging an anti-communist campaign, so these two become a dream team, as neither worries about trampling constitutional rights.

Many Americans in the 1950s sympathize with communist or "leftist" ideals, which they believe echo the principals upon which this country was founded: liberty, equality, and justice for all. But McCarthy accuses anyone with communist sympathies of being part of a "Red Menace" bent on overthrowing the U.S. government.

McCarthy's crusade is a reign of terror that destroys lives. Americans are fired from jobs, alienated from their families, forced to spy on and betray friends, hounded by the FBI, hauled before congressional tribunals such as the House Un-American Activities Committee, and jailed for their political beliefs. Two are executed. Their children, called Red Diaper Babies, are taunted with cries such as "Commies! Go back to Russia! The only good Red's a dead Red!"

New legislation makes it illegal for anyone to write, print, teach, or display materials that advocate overthrowing the U.S. government, or to be a member of a group that produces such materials. Members of the Communist Party USA and members of any alleged communist front organization must register with the newly established Subversive Activities Control Board.

President Truman issues an executive order that ushers in mandatory loyalty oaths. Proof of disloyalty to the United States is not necessary. Mere suspicion is enough to fire a government employee. Universities and businesses follow this example, often dismissing employees based on the flimsiest of allegations.

Enter Julius and Ethel Rosenberg, a leftist-leaning couple who are accused of passing secret information about atomic bomb technology to the Soviets. The Rosenbergs are tried, convicted, and sentenced to death with scant evidence and false testimony.

People around the world, including Pope Pius XII, protest this injustice. At home, Americans are divided. Many call the Rosenbergs innocent martyrs in the cause of political freedom. Others dub them traitors. In the midst of widespread fear and hysteria, there is no middle ground—no moderate position between proclaiming the Rosenbergs' complete innocence, and insisting that the Rosenbergs are guilty of treason and deserve execution.

Appeals wend through the courts for three years until all options are exhausted. On June 19, 1953, a month before the Korean War ends, first Julius Rosenberg, and then Ethel minutes later, are each strapped into the electric chair at Sing Sing. They leave behind two young sons, Michael and Robert.

So . . . if these boys could lose their parents to the anti-communism hysteria, what stops the same thing from happening to any other child's parents?

Nothing.

Transcripts of Russian documents and tapes released in 1995 yield evidence that Julius Rosenberg was indeed a Soviet agent who passed some information to the USSR. No evidence implicates Ethel Rosenberg. In fact, grand jury transcripts released in 2008 reveal that she was *not* involved in passing secrets to the Soviets. She was guilty of only two things: political idealism and loyalty to her husband, with whom she went to her death rather than betray him.

What became of Joseph McCarthy? The Senate voted to censure—formally condemn—him for contempt and abuse of his position. He died in 1957, at age forty-nine.

His name, and the term *McCarthyism*, outlive him in infamy, serving as a warning to people who cherish constitutional safeguards.

ACKNOWLEDGMENTS

An insightful editor/collaborator is invaluable, and I deeply appreciate Amy Fitzgerald and the people at Lerner Publishing Group, who've given this book a healthy home. I am grateful to the many "Red Diaper Babies," especially the Rosenberg/Meeropol family, for interviews, videos, and books about their lives during and since the McCarthy era. I lived this story as a child and have been writing it, in one way or another, all my life. I thank my sweet husband, Tom Ruby, for patiently enduring this obsession with me and for challenging me with just the right questions that I wasn't always graceful about hearing. Many thanks, as well, to my three sons, David, Kenn, and Jeff, who drew me out to those miserably hot Kansas baseball fields summer after summer, and who constantly talked sports at our dinner table until baseball seeped its way into my pores. Evan, I'll catch you on another book, but for this one, I want to acknowledge two of my grandsons, Jacob and Max, for giving me a glimpse into what being a twelve-year-old, Midwestern, sports-loving kid is all about.

TOPICS FOR DISCUSSION

1. Why is the Rosenbergs' case such a big deal for the country? Why does it feel especially important to Marty?

2. Why does Marty write memos to Mickey Mantle? How does doing this help him deal with his problems throughout the novel?

3. What problems do Marty's parents have with Senator McCarthy and FBI director Hoover?

4. Marty has to do bomb drills in school. What dangers do you and your classmates prepare for in school? How are they similar to or different from an atomic bomb attack?

5. The Rafners are singled out by their neighbors because of their suspected communist sympathies. What do you think is the most upsetting thing someone does to Marty or his parents?

6. Marty wonders, "Can you be a patriotic American and a communist at the same time?" What do you

think? Now think of other words you could substitute for "communist." What types of beliefs or backgrounds scare people today the way communism scared people in the 1950s?

7. Why does Marty's mom refuse to name other people who might be communists in order to get herself out of trouble?

8. Why does Luke hate the bugle?

9. Marty is frustrated with his mom for putting the family in danger and scared about the consequences of her actions. When does he decide he's also proud of her, and why?

10. Why does Luke go up to the top of the Tower? How does Marty convince him to come down?

11. Why does Marty agree to go to the vigil for the Rosenbergs, even though he says, "It won't change a thing"?

12. Do you think Marty and Connor will become real friends again? Why or why not?

ABOUT THE AUTHOR

Lois Ruby is a former librarian and the author of 20 books for young readers. She divides her time among family, community social action, research, writing, and visiting schools to energize young people about the ideas in books and the joys of reading. Lois lives in Albuquerque and shares her life with her psychologist husband, Dr. Tom Ruby, as well as their three sons and daughters-in-law and seven amazing grandchildren, who are scattered around the country.